2012

010
1
010

1

2 9 NOV 2012

Adèle

Adèle

Jane Eyre's Hidden Story

Emma Tennant

**Thorndike Press • Chivers Press
Waterville, Maine USA Bath, England**

This Large Print edition is published by Thorndike Press®, USA and by Chivers Press, England.

Published in 2003 in the U.S. by arrangement with William Morrow, an imprint of HarperCollins Publishers, Inc.

Published in 2003 in the U.K. by arrangement with HarperCollins Inc.

U.S. Hardcover 0-7862-5326-6 (Women's Fiction Series)
U.K. Hardcover 0-7540-1949-7 (Windsor Large Print)
U.K. Softcover 0-7540-9310-7 (Paragon Large Print)

The text of this Large Print edition is unabridged.
Other aspects of the book may vary from the original edition.

Set in 16 pt. Plantin by Myrna S. Raven.

Printed in the United States on permanent paper.

British Library Cataloguing-in-Publication Data available

Library of Congress Cataloging-in-Publication Data

Tennant, Emma.
  Adèle : Jane Eyre's hidden story / Emma Tennant.
    p. cm.
  ISBN 0-7862-5326-6 (lg. print : hc : alk. paper)
  1. Eyre, Jane (Fictitious character) — Fiction.
2. Abandoned children — Fiction. 3. Guardian and ward — Fiction. 4. Governesses — Fiction. 5. England — Fiction. 6. Girls — Fiction. 7. Large type books.
  I. Brontë, Charlotte, 1816–1855. Jane Eyre. II. Title.
PR6070.E52A66 2003
  823′.914—dc21   2003041653

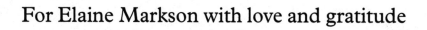

For Elaine Markson with love and gratitude

Preface

In Charlotte Brontë's novel *Jane Eyre* there lives a little French girl, Adèle. Jane was her governess at Thornfield Hall.

Brought over from Paris by Edward Rochester, the eight-year-old Adèle was saved from the danger and miseries of a child alone on the streets of Europe's most corrupt and decadent capital. Her mother, circus trapeze artist and comedy actress Céline Varens, had abandoned her and run off to Italy with a musician. Adèle had nowhere to go.

Whether life is better for the eight-year-old at Thornfield Hall than it was in France is hard to say. England — and the moors surrounding the old house — seemed cold and foreign to Adèle. And there's the added terror of finding a secret existence at the Hall, in the attic and out on the battlemented roof.

For Adèle Varens, the child who comes to Thornfield as Mr. Rochester's ward, uncovers a hidden history in the fabric of Thornfield Hall.

The story opens in Paris, in Adèle's time

before her world changes and falls apart —
and before she meets Jane Eyre, the young
woman who will eventually be her governess and savior.

Here are Jane Eyre's words, in the con-
cluding section of Charlotte Brontë's
novel, on the subject of Adèle:

You have not quite forgotten little
Adèle, have you, reader? I had not; I
soon asked and obtained leave of Mr.
Rochester, to go and see her at the
school where he had placed her. Her
frantic joy at beholding me again
moved me much. She looked pale and
thin: she said she was not happy. I
found the rules of the establishment
were too strict, its course of study too
severe for a child of her age: I took her
home with me. I meant to become her
governess once more, but I soon found
this impracticable; my time and cares
were now required by another — my
husband needed them all. So I sought
out a school conducted on a more in-
dulgent system, and near enough to
permit of my visiting her often, and
bringing her home sometimes. I took
care she should never want for anything
that could contribute to her comfort:

she soon settled in her new abode, became very happy there, and made fair progress in her studies. As she grew up, a sound English education corrected in a great measure her French defects; and when she left school, I found in her a pleasing and obliging companion: docile, good-tempered, and well-principled. By her grateful attention to me and mine, she has long since well repaid any little kindness I ever had it in my power to offer her.

FROM *Jane Eyre* by CHARLOTTE BRONTË

But perhaps, as is often found in the lives of girls as they grow into women, it was all a little more complicated than that.

This is Adèle's story.

Part One

One

Adèle

Tomorrow is the Pierrot in our pantomimes.

All facts look so much the more like fairy stories because, in our time, fairy stories take unconscionable pains to look like the truth.
— BALZAC, *Cousin Pons*

We lived in Paris, in a house on a long, gloomy street, the rue Vaugirard in Montparnasse, but our house was far from being somber or sad. There were three stories: the maid Bettina under the eaves, with a little child's bedroom next to it that I seldom occupied, as Maman allowed me to sleep on the chaise in the sitting room next to the pretty bedroom she had to herself. On the first floor lived old Tante Irène, who some said was the cousin of Herr Graff, whose house this really was — he who made a fortune from promoting the railroads in Baden. But in reality Tante Irène was a milliner, and I would search for scraps for her all day: a feather from the park for a hat for the Comtesse Popinot, a twist of silk from Jenny's latest costume (Jenny was Jenny Colon, the famous actress). She was Maman's best friend, and when she came to visit, she would laugh at the new conservatory. This was on the ground floor, just off what had once been a dingy little salon with no space for more than a table and four chairs: "Céline Varens!" Jenny would cry in astonishment — though of course you couldn't tell whether she was in earnest or not. "*Ma chère* Céline! Has the milord from England bought you this? How many francs did this cost to erect, I ask you?" And she would sweep around the glorious ballroom of glass, with its pink frosted chandelier and the parrot shrieking on its perch. "When is he coming to take you to his castle, *ma chérie?* One thing is certain, you can't take this contraption with you — the frost in *Angleterre* would crack it and the snow would come drifting in!" And Jenny, making a scene so realistic of the glass igloo where my mother would be forced to live that we'd both shiver in the heat of a Parisian afternoon, would go off into more peals of laughter. She was afraid, I believe, that she would lose Maman to the country over the gray sea — but I didn't like to think of her going there, and, with a regularity that must have been tiresome to both friends, I burst into tears at this point, and Maman was forced to lay her finger over her lips. She and Jenny weren't in the profession for nothing, however, and they'd mime the life Céline would be subjected to if she went to this fabulous castle in the north of a cold country — picking icicles from the windows, throwing around their shoulders the cashmere shawls the milord sent Maman from his travels to India, and making a pretense of building a fire in the little paved garden beyond the walls of the conservatory.

For all their clowning, I couldn't be persuaded to smile. I didn't know the milord — though Maman told me I'd met him when I was very small. I knew I never wanted to meet him — "*Cher* Edouard," as Jenny mockingly named my mother's protector and lover of times gone by. Then she'd set off for the theater. Like Maman, Jenny could turn her hand to most kinds of acting and singing, whether vaudeville or *opéra comique*. But only Maman, the beautiful and famous Céline Varens, daughter of the old Funambules Theater before it was transformed, *danseuse de corde* — tightrope walker many leagues in the air —

could master all of them. Maman could sing like a nightingale, and she could play the great tragic roles as well. She would be Phèdre, pacing the glass cage the new conservatory now became — waiting for her young lover, and I the incestuous stepson Hippolyte. How proud I was of Maman! There was literally no one like her — for it was impossible to know what she would next be like.

Our days in Paris, so far as the changing nature of her roles permitted, followed a pattern of which I never tired. After a morning in the sunny glass room, banked high with roses and freesias from Maman's admirers, we would abandon the attempt at lessons (I was supposed to learn English, but the thick, ugly language stuck in my mouth like unchewed meat) and set off for the park. It might be the Luxembourg Gardens, neat and yet with secret twists and turns, box hedges and laurel cut in half-human shapes, so that Maman would bow gravely, feigning acquaintance with a topiary bush. Passersby would stare at us, and of this I was also proud, for I knew by their gaze that I was pretty, too, and that my good looks accentuated Maman's. Sometimes a man would say in a hushed voice to his companion, "Surely that must be Céline Varens!" and I would be prouder still. I was the spitting image of my mother — so Jenny and all Maman's friends said. On our outings to the park, walking the dark length of rue Vaugirard to the Luxembourg Gardens, I glowed in the knowledge that I wore the same dress — pale blue like forget-me-knots, with rose pantalettes — as the celebrated Céline Varens. "Madame is today, mademoiselle is tomorrow," said our dandy, a *flâneur* or boulevard walker known slightly to Maman; a man who searched endlessly for novelty and amusement. And Paris could provide them: I loved to feel, in those moments, a part of the great city, the capital of luxury. I loved to be tomorrow, walking always a few feet behind today. Little did I know then the cruel pantomime I would be coerced into making come true.

When my mother was in a piece at the Funambules Theater, I would go and watch — a panto or a fairy-tale play, as they called them — and whichever one of Maman's admirers was in attendance at the time would carry me right up to the gods, the seats high in the roof of the old theater in the boulevard du Temple. I was spoiled, I knew it — but her lovers knew

17

they must please me if they were to win the love of my mother — and what I knew and they knew made for a kind of laughing friendship between us with the young men (they were invariably younger than Maman, though I didn't know it then) vying with one another to buy me ice cream made from pistachio nuts, or lollipops with the face of Pierrot painted on, or whatever novelty I craved. They knew, too, that they were as much a passing fancy for Maman as the new Italian ices were for me, and as quick to melt away. I was in love with the sad man with the tragic, kohl-rimmed eyes, who was a figure of fun, romantic, and pathetic: the great Pierrot of Paris, Dubureau. He would bow for me alone, in his white clown's costume staring first up at "paradise," where he knew me to be installed, and then down at his feet, clad in slippers with pom-poms of red and blue. And Maman's admirers knew that she was in love with no one, counting Jenny Colon as her great friend and confidante and needing nothing from a man. So I was foolish enough to believe at the time. "Adèle, I trust you to follow me in more ways than one," my mother said to me when she saw the admiring glances of the men of the Funambules at the pretty pic-

18

ture we made together. "I expect you to go as far as I have" — and she gestured at the stage and the rope where she danced nightly, slung at an audacious height between two poles — "even further, *ma chérie,* for my greatest wish is for my child to become a true actress . . . to play in Corneille and Racine . . . like the great Rachel." And before I could ask her more about these grand-sounding names, Maman had swept away to her dressing room — or to dinner with a new suitor. It was rare for the famous Céline Varens to speak to me directly — so, thinking of those days, it seems to me. She loved to kiss and fondle, and then she would set me down again with a preoccupied air. I suppose I was too young then to understand her ambitions for me — but I knew I adored it when she called me her *chérie.*

Pierrot was my friend and understood my tears and tantrums, and when the show was over (the month I'm thinking of is April, and Maman would run to her dressing room to change before taking me backstage to see Jenny in the *opéra comique;* she was starring in *Piquillo*), I hugged Pierrot and said good night before we set off. Everything about the evening was fine and full of promise, a Paris evening that has its blue hour, the hour my other friend Félix calls "between dog and wolf," and when he says it, he looks at my mother and laughs. For there is something unlikely about a woman as beautiful as Céline — Félix compares her to a heroine painted by Delacroix, and with her dark hair in ringlets at her neck and her flashing black eyes she could lead a battalion into war — there was perhaps something a little strange about the fact that Maman professed to be perfectly happy living alone with her daughter and a fussy old woman like Tante Irène when she could have the world's most exciting city at her feet. "Céline loves no new man as much as her new conservatory," Jenny says, laughing as Félix does, and she comes to pick me up and carry me to bed on the chaise with the rose cretonne coverlet, in the room next to Maman's.

If Pierrot was silent, as he must be, with all life's tragedy expressed in those kohl-rimmed eyes and sad, springing walk, then Félix never stopped talking, and he loved to talk to me. Especially today: we're going to the *foire du pain d'épice* together, the fair where they sell bread spiced with cloves and nutmeg and poppy seeds, all my favorites, and a sign that Easter, the time of year Maman loved best, was coming soon. Félix is a genius, and I'm proud to be seen with him when he's talking, so concentrated and solemn. We've spent some time in his studio, the garret room where Félix makes his pictures on the quai des Grands Augustins, and we're walking fast to Saint-Germain. I smelled the hot, spicy bread already, and I'm pretending that what happened in Félix's studio hasn't taken place at all. For Félix — who makes pictures of real people, not with paint but with a machine that takes their exact likeness and after that he plunges the likeness into a bath of strong-smelling stuff I am never allowed to go near — has shown me a picture I don't want to see at all. "It's a process known as wet-collodion," Félix says as we stride along. "Your father has come out well, don't you think? Now take care of it — Maman will find you a frame."

If Pierrot was thin and curved, like a crescent moon in his white clown's suit, then here's another contrast with my good friend Félix — for Nadar, as he's known by all the poets and painters who come to have their faces stolen by him, is large and bulky. He's a giant who seems to take up most of the street, and today, with his great head looming above a shapeless brown coat and a cravat that's all over the place because he hasn't bothered to tie it properly, he looks like nothing so much as one of his own daguerreotypes — or whatever name he gives the new invention, the "wet-collodion" plate he boasts of these days. He looks only partly developed, with a brush of hair that could be a swirl of the brown chemical that has his landlady threatening eviction from the room high under the eaves in the rue de l'Ancienne Comédie.

Today I find I have as little to say to him in reply as I would to the image, frowning, half apologetic, of the madman Félix has recently put on his plate, Monsieur de Nerval. I can no more ask for an explanation of those dreadful words "your father" from Félix Nadar than I could from the lunatic poet who walks his pet lobster in the gardens of the Tuileries, the man they say has verse coming out of his head like the water in the great stone fountains there. I'm walking with a stranger, now the subject of close family has been raised: doesn't Félix know that no one ever mentions a father — or an Englishman — in our house? And that Tante Irène, when she made some witticism about hats *à l'anglais,* was severely reprimanded by Jenny, who looks after Maman's sensibilities as if they were

22

her own. Even then, with Jenny scolding and Maman red-eyed (though I refused to admit this), it never occurred to me that I did have a father, and that he is an Englishman. "I am on the verge of a revolution, a great invention," Félix says joyously, having noticed nothing at all of my new sulky mood. "Come, we'll go to the place de la Nation," he adds when my silence begins to alarm him, "the fair where they sell gingerbread and honey, eh, Adèle?" But before I have time to decide I like him again, Félix is back with his wet-collodion plate and his impression of Théophile Gautier, which a satirical magazine will attempt to reproduce. "People will be grateful one day," the good Nadar enthuses. "They will say Félix Nadar was inventor of a new science of memory — what do you think of that, child?"

The truth was, I had no wish for a science of memory, and least of all for a discipline that would re-create memories of a man I had no interest in at all. Félix couldn't know I carried the picture of a face I didn't recognize and had determined never to look at closely again, purely out of friendship for this old family friend. Once I was home, I would throw it in the deep basket where Tante Irène discards the scraps of silk and taffeta, the trimmed violet petals and fabric twigs for a corsage ordered by the "actresses," as Maman's female acquaintances like to be known. The frowning visage of a man to whom I bore no kind of relation in my heart would then be carried to the municipal rubbish dump and burned. Maman would never know that her longtime companion Félix had brought the man who had caused her great unhappiness (this much I could and did know) right into her home.

However, hard as I tried, I couldn't make that day just before Easter go well. I said I didn't want to go to the big fair in the place de la Nation — and this had Félix staring down at me, for the first time genuinely worried. I wanted to go home and dispose of this new invention, the evidence of my paternity. I saw myself, eyes closed, consigning the angry, darkly shadowed face — which reminded me of nothing so much as the illustration for Bluebeard, in my book of Perrault's fairy tales — to Tante Irène's willow basket. Then I would go and curl up next to my mother in the glass conservatory, where the jasmine and orchids sent by admirers made a heady scent like summer. I wanted to discuss our next trip — out to Versailles, perhaps, or to the races where Maman and I, dressed in identical costumes, would cheer the win of the vicomte's fine gray. The vicomte was the latest handsome Frenchman to succumb to the charms of the famous and lovely Céline Varens. I like to portray the admirers in this way, like the gossip columnists do when they write about Maman and Jenny Colon — though they sneer at Jenny's strange admirer, the poet Gérard de Nerval, with his lobster on a blue ribbon when he comes to call. He left a parrot as a gift for us at the door once, and Monsieur Punch now lives in the conservatory, speaking in mincing tones like the vicomte when he pleases or shrieking like de Nerval himself.

Today, as I say, has decided to be different. I come along the rue Vaugirard, say good-bye to Félix — who I can see is as relieved as I am that I don't want to go off in pursuit of gingerbread, for he wants only to race back to his portraits — and I enter the house by the side door into the little paved garden. The portrait of the frowning man, deep within my pocket, cuts my leg as I walk, hard and sharp, and I can't wait to get rid of it forever. Even Monsieur Punch's cheerful call from his perch within the conservatory doesn't stop me from frowning, too, and I run up to the door from the greenhouse into the square of garden, perpetually in shadow, on which Monsieur Graff threatens to build an extension, thus ruining my and Maman's heavenly times alone together. But Jenny says she'll see to it that he never will.

"So this is our *petit bijou*," a voice says as I open the door and run in. "I congratulate you, Céline. You have educated the child to look very like you in the face."

My mother is half sitting, half lying on a cane chaise at the side of the conservatory. My first impression is that she's very posed, more so even than when Nadar tried to "capture" her on one of his strange-smelling plates. She looks beautiful — but nervous. She's in a sky blue chenille gown that the vicomte says makes her look like an angel. "Not since we were at the villa together," says the man I don't dare look up at. He's in an upright chair and holds a whip with a gold handle — which reminds me, though I know Maman would be furious if I said this, of the ringmaster at the Hippodrome, when she and Jenny take me to the circus for my winter treat. He sounds amused but contemptuous at the same time. I know I hate this man. And I know, too, though of course he cannot know it, that I carry his image in the pocket of my rose pantalettes: I own him, just as, from his odious assumption that I am his and Maman's "little jewel," he appears to be certain he owns me. In my heart I leave the house forever — but then the picture of my desolate mother returns to haunt me, and I creep back, in the cold gray dawn, to the house in the rue Vaugirard. "Well, speak up, little Adèle," the stranger says in a voice that doesn't even attempt to be kind.

If Félix has taught me that even the tallest and burliest of men can have hearts of gold, then Pierrot, the clown who lies in order to demonstrate the truth at the core of things, has instructed me in the way mime can lead the audience astray and convince them of the opposite of what they expect. I run on tiptoe, all little-girl smiles and dimples, to the man in the green velvet jacket in the high-backed chair near where Maman, suddenly an invalid, lies. I lift my cheek to be kissed; my hands fly out behind me, like a tiny ballerina's. All the while the paper with its print from Nadar's prized wet-collodion plate bites into my thigh and nearly causes me to scream. But, like Pierrot, I am silent — and only Monsieur Punch, who has been trained by the

27

poet Gérard to mouth obscenities in the tongue of an extinct Amazonian tribe, gives vent to his incredulity at my behavior. "That's better," says the visitor, whose breath reeks of tobacco — and something else, too, something sweet and sickly and strong. "So you do remember our times in the white villa by the blue sea, you little monkey, the house with the steps right down to the water, eh?"

Nadar, my friend who came to our house sometimes when Maman was away in the provinces, performing in circus tents pegged on dry grass — on hot summer nights when I missed her most of all, lonely in the stifling small rooms at home — Nadar would tell me that I had just as much love in me as everyone else. "Yours is bottled up, Adèle, and you must not permit it to turn sour," he said. And he looked almost sad as he spoke. "You are an actress like your mother, *ma petite,* and like her you will receive blows as you go through life. But don't become a cynic — after all, Céline never has."

I didn't know what the word meant, but I ran to the giant Nadar and reached out my arms so he could lift me high in the room and make me queen of the fussy household Jenny loved to preside over: the

round tables with their collections of bibe-
lots and enameled snuffboxes; the
Récamier bed, resplendent in its uphol-
stery of salmon velvet. "I am *not* — what
you say" — I whispered in his ear, and
then we both burst out laughing, though I
went on to shed tears at this understanding
on Nadar's part of my need for love and
my desire to give it. For it is true, I feel
this bottled-up sensation sometimes, and I
know that my mimicry and precious airs
come to me as a guard against my real,
true love. Nadar it is who saves me from
the bad parts of myself. But Nadar, as I
know too well, is not here with me today.
And the strong effect the stranger's words
about his white villa by the blue sea have
had on me will have to go unexplained
until I see my friend again.

At this point — and just as I was noticing the fact that this dark, ugly stranger
held my mother's whip in his hand, the elegant little whip that had been her mother's
and grandmother's, the whip with the Jap-
anese inlaid handle and streamer of blue
ribbon, employed by Céline's family of acrobats and trainers since the early days of
the Funambules Theater — the door
leading to the inner salon opened, and
Jenny came in. She must have seen me

reaching out for the fine-thonged whip, which had tamed so many of the horses and ponies Céline's grandmother rode bareback on a circle of hot sand, standing tall while the tightrope walkers swayed above them. Jenny looked around the scented, overfurnished conservatory, and I saw she was angry. I also saw she hates the man who both pushes me away and drew me onto his knee: she pulled me from him abruptly and set me down in the salon, with a warning that I'd be put to bed without a visit from Maman if I didn't go straight up to my room and settle myself down instantly. The whip, I saw to my surprise (later, when I looked back on this scene: Maman prostrate and pink in the face, the visitor both abashed and arrogant, I wondered at her permitting him to take it from the glass cabinet where, along with other paraphernalia of circus days, it was proudly displayed), the whip was handed to Jenny, by the man I refused to accept as my father, and replaced. I heard the door of the cabinet close as I went up the stairs, dragging my feet. But I was afraid Jenny would catch me and vent this new anger on me, so I arrived in the little chamber at the top of the stairs and climbed into bed without a murmur. It was a long time since I'd tried to go to sleep in the room designated as mine when Céline was first given "this charming hotel," as she had said of the house in rue Vaugirard. Bettina the maid was out, Tante Irène on the floor below closed in with her feathers and artificial flowers and unable to hear me if I cried for company. I had spent too long on the chaise next to my mother's room. That evening I had the first premonition that Maman might leave me (though there was no reason to suppose this; I knew she had arranged within the past week to sing with a new musician, whose opera would be staged at the theater), and I suffered a devastation of loneliness that appeared to me, in my ever-growing distress, to presage a future that would be unbearably different from the past.

I hadn't lain there for more than an hour (though it seemed an age to me) when a light step on the stair announced Maman herself, contrite and breathless, as if she had been saving up all the things she wanted to say to me and realized she must speak soon before I lost my trust in her. "Adèle, are you awake?" Her voice was low and uncertain, and I felt a tremor of apprehension run through me: was the announcement of a long journey abroad about to be made? Buenos Aires, or the fabulous East — I had heard Maman and Jenny dream aloud, on evenings when hard gray rain came down on the roof of the conservatory. Paris was the same gray wherever you looked. They would go without me, I knew, to the green jungles where Monsieur Punch's family of parrots darted between tall trees. I would be left alone, with Maman's friends looking in to the house in rue Vaugirard less and less often now that the woman they all loved was no longer there.

"Yes, I'm awake, Maman," I replied. "What time is it?" And I pretended, by yawning and slowly opening and closing my eyes, that I had been asleep all along.

"It's not late," Maman said, "not for you anyway — and I am sorry you were sent upstairs, *ma chérie*. But things are not so easy here always, you know. . . ." And here her voice tailed off, and she fell silent.

I know — this is what I wished to say, but my mother spoke again in a rush of words I had never heard from her before. "I have my work, and I have my child" — here she reached out and took my hand, and I felt her fingers strong and slim against mine. "And there are those who like to take Céline Varens to dinner or to a box at the opera, for the pleasure of watching the reaction of the crowd."

"*Maman est belle,*" I said — and I knew as I spoke that my mother's beauty meant little to her, and that she wished to tell me what really lay in her heart.

"There is one man who cannot leave me — though he does, very often, return to his life and estates across the sea."

"Do you love him, Maman?" I heard my voice cry out in alarm. And — fatally — "When will the milord leave again? I hope he will go soon. . . ."

"He wishes me to leave with him," my mother replied, and her voice was tight with the hurt I had just inflicted on her. "But Paris holds all my friends, my theater" — and here, forgiven as I always was, I found myself scooped up and hugged and kissed — "and *ma petite* Adèle. She is happy here with me, *non?*"

"Yes, yes," I whispered, still held close to the soft, powdered cheek of Céline. "Happy here . . ."

So it was, when my mother had kissed me a hundred times more and had run down the stairs again, that I felt secure in the knowledge of her love and in the continuation of our life together. Everything would go on being exactly the same. So, as I tried to lull myself into a real sleep, I taught myself to believe.

Inevitably, as I lay in the minute four-poster with its rosy coverlet and muslin hangings, I now found myself transported to that realm — the past — that my busy, happy life had obliterated up until now. I saw myself on a path with bushes that bore yellow flowers but were prickly to the touch, and from the path I came to a flight of shallow stone steps, these bordered by the same profusion of gorse and broom. The steps led downward — to my childish eye there seemed to be a hundred of them — and at the base, as far away and tiny as the painted glass of a scene trapped in a dome (I owned one of these, a Paris snow-storm, Notre Dame blanketed with fine white flakes at the toss of a hand), lay the sea. I had never seen the sea in my life, and I stopped dead in my tracks. It was my misfortune also to turn and look behind me. I felt alone in this great empty land-scape, with water stretching to the horizon.

A white villa — I have heard Maman speak of it sometimes, so I know this is where we went that summer when I can have been no more than two or three years old — stood proudly at the top of the path.

Palm trees and an orange grove partly obscured it from view, and a fine heat haze caused it to shimmer like a palace in a fairy tale. Unsure whether to press ahead in the direction of the vast enigma of the sea or to retrace my steps, I stood rooted to the spot, my eyes fixed behind me on the figure of the man now visible as he descended the roughest part of the path and made for the flight of stone stairs.

The man was my father. Maman had spent the last day since we arrived teaching me to say "Papa" (a word I somehow knew would make Jenny show her contempt). And this strange man with whom I was instructed to be so familiar was naked on the narrow path. He stooped, caught by my grave regard in the act of dropping his breeches, and I saw he held in his hand a pair of trunks into which he now proceeded to thrust a pair of hairy legs. He muttered something, which sounded like an apology. Then, "What are you doing out here on your own, little one?" And he came forward to lift me and ran with great, lurching steps down the flight of stairs to a flat rock that jutted out into the sea. Here my screams prevented him from diving in with me headfirst, and Maman, who sat perched up above the rock with a parasol held high in the air, called out for my release. But I felt that this cowardice on my part turned the ugly man against me, and sure enough, later when I lay in my bed at the villa, listening to the wind in the pines at the back of the house, I heard Maman pleading for me, with this stranger who carried something like a cudgel between his legs, for this I had seen on the path. "Let her stay here, Edouard," came the voice of the woman who was the toast of Paris, the beautiful opera dancer Céline Varens. I squirmed at the piteous tone she employed in begging to keep me in the white villa by the sea. I had never heard Maman speak like this before, and I didn't know it was the voice of abasement and love.

Until this evening I had forgotten the ugly man and his nakedness, the tears of my mother, and the great pine with its umbrella branches soughing in the wind at the back of the house. But now, as I wait hour after hour for Maman to mount the stairs and tell me the coast is clear and I can return to the chaise in her boudoir and at last find comfort and sleep, it all returns to me with the black-inked certainty of one of Félix's portraits of a frozen past. I must have dropped off to sleep in the end, I suppose, for it is morning and a bright Easter sun comes through the curtains. I run down to the boudoir — there is no one there — and then to the salon, which smells of Jenny's café au lait, as always. Here is Jenny on her own: the house in rue Vaugirard is empty, and Jenny says Maman has gone to the theater early, to rehearse. The man who came last night isn't mentioned at all. Apart from a lingering whiff of tobacco in the conservatory, there is no sign he ever *was* here. Félix's portrait of him I had not in the end thrown away; instead I had stowed it in the little chest in my bedroom where I keep my secret things.

Two

"The eighteenth card illustrates the dark realm of Hecate, the night hag. The sign of the Crab, seventh sign of the zodiac, emblem of the primitive forces of the unconscious. Here are the stone pillars of Hades, gateway of life and death; reigning over all is the moon. This is the critical stage of the journey, where existence hangs in the balance. . . ."

The speaker, an old woman Maman and Jenny call simply La Cibot, looks at me as she pronounces, and I can see that Maman isn't pleased by this at all. It's the first time the *fillette* of the actress and opera singer Céline Varens and her devoted friend Jenny Colon (everyone always behaved as if I were somehow their daughter, and I had long accepted it) has been allowed to come into the shabby street deep in the Marais where the fortune-teller plies her trade. So how can it be that someone so young, so clearly without an interesting future for several years yet, can command the attentions of the crone?

Maman coughs as Jenny, taking a

morning away from the theater and preparations of *Piquillo*, lights up a cheroot and leans back in her chair, placing her legs in a ringmaster's pair of tan leather boots right up on the table where La Cibot lays out her tarot pack. A black hen named Cleopatra nibbles at seeds under the table, and a toad with a long biblical name no one can pronounce sits up close to the cards, with their crudely colored pictures of towers, hanged men, and malevolent moons.

I am not afraid of La Cibot — she's come to the rue Vaugirard too often to occasion alarm — and I've heard Maman and Jenny joke about her unsuccessful predictions as I drop off to sleep, comfortable in the knowledge that one thing is fixed in my life and that is the happiness of living forever with my adored mother. I've only been allowed to come along because I begged to — the Italian lessons Maman has suddenly decided I need are boring me, and the woman with the loud, theatrical voice, the sister of the new musician-director at the Funambules who comes to teach me this language Maman says I will be grateful one day to know, has developed a bad Parisian cold. "I'll be quiet," I told Maman as we set off from the house, Monsieur Punch shouting an imprecation in the new tongue in which I'm supposed to become fluent. "I won't say a word, Maman. You won't know I'm there!" And now it happens that, as far as the old witch is concerned, no one but me is in the fetid little room, with the black hen strutting and pecking under a seldom-cleaned, tasseled cloth and the shutters tightly closed against an early-summer sun. Maman and Jenny might be women without any prospects of romance, fortune, or whatever soothsayers are visited in order to provide; I am, unwittingly and quite undeservingly, the star of the show.

"The tower," intones La Cibot, who has gone into one of her trances (on no account, Jenny has told me, must she be woken until it is time: her heart might stop with the shock of reentering the world we all inhabit). "The tower and the crab together. The journey under the moon." And she fixes on me, from the depths of her hallucinatory state, a gaze so wild and full of foreboding that, for the first time, I feel a real fear on confronting La Cibot. Maman, too, is looking at me anxiously. Why must I go? And where is this dreadful tower? Without warning, the tears come: like a baby I sniffle and gulp, watching a trail of liquid run from my nose down onto my freshly starched pinafore. La Cibot is condemning me to exile; I sense she is sending me away from Maman. It doesn't occur to me at this stage that the ancient fortune-teller may be in on Maman's new plans and has either been told or genuinely picked up from the tarot the fact of our coming separation. How could I imagine such a thing? But in the light of successive events it seems probable La Cibot knew a portion at least of the trouble Maman now finds herself in; and if I had been old enough to think clearly about what the re-percussions of the night before were likely to be, I would have been less surprised by the old witch's pronouncements.

This morning, as we walked along the boulevard Saint-Germain, there had been an atmosphere of joy and plenty. *Flâneurs* — those who simply stroll and observe — went past, enjoying pavement scenes in pausing at cafés where every subject under the sun was aired (and every pocket eyed for the picking) and women in striped jackets and gathered skirts and pretty shoes showing slender ankles in stockings of dyed cotton all gossiped happily. I had seen that Maman alone had been preoccu-pied and even grumpy. My calls to her to look up and admire the chestnut trees with their magnificent candles to grace a poor man's ball, chandeliers lit by a May morning, had gone unheard. Even Jenny, striding along at her side, made no effort to cheer Maman, something she invariably did when her spirits were low. It was as if this capital of the world, this magical city, had lost its allure for one of its greatest gems, the beautiful and celebrated Céline Varens. Yet we were going to La Cibot as if to a doctor, to hear a highly unwelcome diagnosis. Despite the fact, as I reminded myself in our progress through the crowd, that the man Céline had once asked me to call Papa had once more vanished from our lives. What more could Maman possibly want?

What had happened was this. The stranger, as I continued to think of the dark, ill-favored man who had come to our house in rue Vaugirard every two or three days between Easter and this month of early summer, appeared to consider himself owner of all he set eyes on. His possessions included my poor Maman and myself. Just as the "milord anglais" — so Jenny referred to him with a short, sneering laugh — brought on each visit an additional item of furniture or valuable piece of glass or painting for the conservatory (for which he had certainly paid) — so I could see my mother's sense of obligation and feelings of oppression and even hatred toward him grow. Myself, counted as a minor adornment to the ménage, the milord stranger would sometimes throw up in the air, exclaiming I was his little *article de Paris*. By this he meant that I signified to him all the frivolities of the city in which he was so ill suited to live. Even at my tender age, I knew an *article de Paris* to mean a feather, or an artificial flower such as Tante Irène stitched on a hat or corsage for the courtesans the milord and others of his kind frequented when the fancy took them. My reaction to these attentions on the part of this arrogant man may well be imagined.

It was therefore a pleasant relief when one day, just as the good weather was setting in, Maman announced to me that we were going to the races at Longchamps together, and the vicomte, thrust into the background by the arrival of the milord, would be our escort for the day. I liked the vicomte: he was ineffectual but polite and never failed to buy me pastries, including the *fraise de bois* tartlets that Jenny considered too expensive to bring into our little household. "I smell the blood of an Englishman," Jenny called after us when we set off in the vicomte's smart crested phaeton for the first important race meeting of the year; and as we looked behind us, we did indeed see the man who called himself my father disembark from an expensive hired vehicle outside our house and look very disgruntled at being told by Bettina that Madame was not at home. To my delight, Maman thought the joke as good as I did and made no attempt to hide the vicomte's head when the good-natured young man twisted half out of his coach to see what we were laughing at. Unfortunately, as I am bound to think in retrospect, it was a mistake on our part not to restrain the vicomte, and things would be very different today if we had.

The day at the races, during which the vicomte made sure I won several louis d'or (these coins he made appear down my nose or out of his sleeve and were referred to as my "winnings"), was as much enjoyed by my mother as myself. She agreed, so great was her renewed fondness for the vicomte, to accompany him to the opera that evening; I was to be dropped at home, where Jenny and Bettina between them would make my supper, read me stories, and put me to bed. This kind of arrangement had happened dozens of times before, and I thought nothing of it. I was secure in the knowledge that Maman would be home before midnight; she might sit in the conservatory awhile if the evening was fine, and then, pausing in the boudoir on her way to her room, she would stoop low and kiss me good night.

Nothing was as I expected when the vicomte's phaeton dropped me back at the rue Vaugirard. A sulky kitchen maid let me in and then disappeared: the house was empty; and after all the excitement of the racecourse, I felt unable to settle down with a drawing pad or a book. I even went out into the street and looked vainly up and down, in the hope that Jenny or even Bettina might be coming back. Of course there was no sign of them. Then I looked up. A man sat on the balcony of the first-floor suite of rooms, these generally kept locked and reserved for the occasional use of Monsieur Graff.

The man was the milord stranger. He had taken possession of the balcony, just as he had over past weeks commandeered each room in the house, not to mention the conservatory. He saw me at once:

"Adèle!" he called out as I ran indoors and went up the stairs as fast as I could, to reach the safety of my room. "Come here, you little monkey. Where's that flirt your Maman, eh? Tell me that!"

I have seen enough of drunkards to know it's best to keep out of their way, and I ducked down the stairs again at the sound of his voice, the dreadful thought having also come to me that the house was indeed empty except for a mad stranger milord, and that he might chase me right up the stairs and kill me like Bluebeard before locking me in a secret room. But the ogre was faster than I, and he pulled me into the room and then out on to the balcony, where he had been sitting eating chocolate-covered almonds. "Here, you're as bad as your mother. You'll do anything for money," this man, the man my mother could no longer bear to refer to as my father, said in a thick voice. "If you won't eat it, let's throw it." And, to my horror, he started to toss the bonbons, these almonds as hard as stones, onto the roof of the greenhouse below. Soon came crashing sounds as the glass broke into a million fragments and then, try as I might to conceal them, my own cries and sobs in the ensuing silence.

There is worse to come. The only way the stranger could be persuaded to stop from throwing more of these costly chocolate missiles down below was if I climbed onto his knee — something he often tried to make me do when he came to call and was always refused. He was sobbing, too; I hardly dare admit it, but, despite the strong, sweet smell on his breath, I pitied him. Perhaps I was intoxicated by the scent he gave off: partly cognac (with which I was familiar from others of Maman's admirers) and partly something else — I smelled it once on Monsieur de Nerval when he came to woo Jenny, if that is the word for his strange mode of behavior. As I say, I felt the first twinge of sympathy for the sad, drunken stranger. Up close he was no more frightening than the Beast in "Beauty and the Beast," a tale that used to terrify me when I was younger. Now I was adult enough to see that he was unhappy, that he missed Maman as I did. But I had no intention, once it grew dark and the milord was sober enough to be guided down the stairs and out into the street, of allowing him to stay. This shocking display of emotion — smashed conservatory and all — must warn my mother finally of the unsuitability of allowing an Englishman into her home.

Alas, things did not turn out as I had planned. Long after it was dark, the carriage I recognized as belonging to the vicomte drew up outside. The stranger, who had been taking long pulls of brandy from a bottle at his side, set me down roughly and leaned over the edge of the balcony. He called to Maman; then his tone changed, and he turned to run down the stairs and — just where I had wished him three hours earlier, but now too late — out into the street. I heard nothing more after a brief, low exchange between two men: the vicomte, as I can only suppose, and the Englishman.

And here we are — Maman, Jenny, and I — returned from the foolish visit to La Cibot and standing in the ruins of Maman's pretty house in rue Vaugirard. For it's not only the conservatory now that is broken up and destroyed. The house itself has been emptied — of everything. The beds have gone, and all the furniture, and the rosy curtains and the Sèvres plates and all the kitchen spoons and forks and knives.

Even Tante Irène has gone, and with her the pins and the bags of soaps and the bunches of artificial Parma violets.

"What shall we do?" Maman asks Jenny in a dull, sad voice. For once Jenny is at a loss for a reply.

Three

Edward

I am a murderer. Under French law, at least. In defense of my honor I have killed. I will never hear her again, or hold in my arms the daughter of freedom who taught me to love slavery. She will turn from me and curl her lip in contempt. "Go back to your cold country — go back, go back!" And, like the cry of the bird that flies over the moor and awaits our guns when August comes, her voice sounds in my ears as I walk about the house, preparing myself for an influx of visitors. Your house and your land are all you Englishmen care for, so the voice goes on, the voice that can take on a hundred shades, become the voice of tragic queen and simple *comédienne,* of *femme savante* or revolutionary heroine. Your castle, your estates . . . Go back . . .

Now I have little to do but wait for death. My life is laid out before me, like the great tessellated marble floor in the Hall of this mansion I never expected to inherit: the banquets, the long spells of solitude, the hunting parties, and the rest. Twice a year I will travel to my more distant farms, then up to Scotland to visit the Duke of This and the Earl of That, listening in long, dark nights to the sound of their wailing bagpipe music against the tumble of brown waterfalls. All my visits will be to foreign places, places foreign to my heart. And on my arm will be a wife more foreign to me than my grande passion, my belle Céline, could ever prove to be.

For I must marry, or I will go mad.

As luck will have it, there will be two arrivals today at Thornfield Hall. One, my intended bride, comes before noon. We shall walk together in the long hazel avenue where the leaves are green and the bleakness of the surrounding countryside concealed. "How I hate the bareness of the place you describe to me!" Céline would cry as we lay together in the white villa by the sea, the mimosa beyond the window a veil of yellow, the bright blossoms dancing with their feathery leaves as if the grim north of my country were no more than a dream. "I will never come and live there with you. Why don't you sell everything and come permanently to France?"

I forget, in my remembering, the young woman who comes today. I place us together in my imagination on a rugged hill, on the acres Céline rightly accuses me of owning, while the people in my poorly farmed heather country are fortunate if they can find enough to eat. (Yet she doesn't mind the diamonds and cashmeres I buy her with the rents from this accursed land, or the railway stock from the great steel tracks that will cross the perimeter of the estate. Nor the lands in Trinidad that supply the fortune squandered on the conservatory in Paris before I destroyed it. Like so many others, this is a subject on which I cannot dwell.)

Where was I — if not with Céline Varens, in the abolished kingdom that once was ours? I am more truly there than here, so why did I not sell all, as she insisted? Why am I in this godforsaken place, as she would doubtless find it? Why, when I saw the old woman on the heath like the witches who appeared to Macbeth at Forres, did I take no heed of her warning — that my lands would claim me in the end and the ghost of my bride would bring me great unhappiness? I was young and strong then: I should have gone. But I stayed, triumphant at my father's and brother's sudden deaths. I had never anticipated riches, yet I could buy any woman I wanted, and all the luxuries she called for. It was heady stuff for a younger son, and I availed myself of the advantages of my new position. For a milord abroad, as I was to find in Italy with Giacinta and in Germany with Clara, is treated as a little king. He is offered all the treasures of Europe. And if the slave trade in which my late father dealt so profitably has now been ruled unlawful, then the women of Europe are well prepared to make up the deficit. They'd sell their souls — with the exception of Céline, of course, with the exception of Céline — to become mistress of Thornfield Hall. Yet I turned them all down, these willing slaves. I returned here alone, a murderer.

It does not fall to many men to dispose of one wife in order to marry another. "You'd better come upstairs, sir," said Grace Poole at dawn on the day I heard my new bride would come. And I woke before her hand touched my shoulder, so great had been my dread at the knowledge of my impending nuptials spreading through the house. Grace would never tell her charge, naturally — but Leah and the other servants: who can say? I had envisaged it often: the chapel, the old Dowager Ingram in her pew, the stately bride I could almost mistake, as I turned impatient from my place by the altar, for the tall, dark woman I had first married.

Then the sudden silence, as strong as the wind on bright October days that sweeps the moor and scatters leaves along the valleys, crisp, unready to die. The silence — then the murmur, the shuffle of feet drawn in, the rush of skirts along the aisle. The red dress, my God, the red dress. It runs like flames, its wearer a line of fire that makes straight for the table where the holy sacrament is laid out. How can I stop her, this woman who haunts the place as the old witch once said she would? But there is no time to lose. "Come up, sir," Grace Poole says. "We must do something before the ladies are here." And I follow Grace, for she is right. We must do something, and do it now.

What can I say, what can I do in expiation for the sins committed first in my name and then by myself, for the thirty pieces of silver, the thirty thousand pounds with which my poor Antoinette bought me? For the money has bought her only a cage, and like a tropical bird she is frozen to her perch, high above the hum of the household she should by rights have organized and controlled. How can I make reparation to a woman who has lost her mind, who suffers and then forgets, grows violent and then despairs, all in a cloud of oblivion — only on occasion shot through with lucid thought? I cannot love her, nor she me. But she will possess me to the end, if I do not marry and lead a life as other men. The Ingram lands adjoin Thornfield Hall. I'll march with you, dear Blanche; we'll grow rich together.

Already, as I climb to the third story of the house where I saw early on in our honeymoon that the poor Creole would have no choice but to spend her days, I am forced once again to recognize the reality of my life — Grace Poole will see to it! There can be neither passion nor light for you, her solemn tread says, as she mounts the last, twisting step; take your dreams of the Frenchwoman and burn them. You need to marry and produce an heir.

It is too late now for me to return to that state of innocence — ignorance, Céline would say — in which I dwelled when my father and brother lived and I had little to look forward to but church or army, refuge or barracks for a younger son. I was reared by beating and neglect; my mother, who died before I grew, was temperamentally incapable of love. My elder brother, Rowland, secure in his inheritance, bullied me pitilessly. I passed my days on the moor, shooting and hunting. "You were reared to kill," Céline said as we sat one day in the garden of the house I built for her, the house where the scents from the mountains of the Alpes-Maritimes lingered until late among the flowers she grew there. "The birds and beasts you slaughtered were born to die a violent death, and you were from birth their executioner." And Céline, seeing me roll my eyes in astonishment at her strange ideas, laughed and rose from the table where we sat over peaches and wine. "One day," she said, "you will understand. When you come to this country to live, and meet those who see the truth and continue the fight for liberty and justice." But these words meant nothing to me then; and now that I understand them, it is too late. I am a murderer and never can return to France. I have no choice but to reflect, as I follow the grim figure of Grace Poole ever upward, that the heiress I betrayed enjoys a brilliant revenge. For even Céline could not have heard the secret of my West Indian marriage. And if she had discovered it, what would she have thought of me then? It is a secret I must carry to the grave — and now the only question is, as I know too well, whether the grave will prove to be Antoinette's or mine.

I cannot give details of my visits to my wife. As ever before, the sheer inhumanity of her treatment appalls me. But money handed over to Grace Poole finds its way to drink and a threatening scowl if I complain. Grace holds my future, as well as my insufferable present, in her hands. No hint of the presence of Bertha, as once I called my wife, can become known. Mrs. F, my housekeeper, is obliging enough to tell visitors a ghost haunts Thornfield Hall; and so indeed it does.

I said I would not describe a visit to my wife, and the reason is simple, though I cannot dare to breathe it, for fear that the contrary of what I found on the third story of my accursed inheritance yet proves the case.

I opened the steel door, the door to which only I possess a key, as Grace stood back, her foul body stink almost overcoming me in the low-ceilinged, narrow passage of the attic. I smelled gin, and the sourness that comes from a diet of cabbage, bread, and little else. It is long since I insisted my Antoinette should eat well, as once we had together, on that island in the Windwards where the breeze blows soft, laden with spices and hibiscus, a feast to stomach, ear, and eye. But Grace disobeys me — she knows she can — and I have suspicions that my poor mad wife goes hungry if she refuses the same dreary diet as her wardress. She is thin enough, God knows. And it was the sight of her I had come to dread more than any other part of my ordeal of a life here at Thornfield Hall. Thin, spectral — she is indeed the ghost of our first days of love. Her floating mind, so desperately seeking for a stable meaning in the world, is the opposite exactly of Céline's — for Céline, whose perfect balance could be savored as she rode bareback or danced across the wire stretched high above the ring, has reason and clarity as her guides, and this starveling, stumbling creature has none. Oh, if I could only have met Céline Varens when I was still young and unmarried! All the plans made by my gold-hungry father would have come to nothing. I would have lived out under the stars, traveling with the little provincial circus Céline loved to work with through the summer months. I would have swept and carried for her, poor as a stable lad.

This is not to the point — nor, as I suspect when the wild longings for my brave actress seize me, would they be believed by such as Grace Poole, who stares suspiciously at me as I walk past her antechamber and into the room with beams as low and dark as the Thornfield forest in which Antoinette always refused to walk. Here I'm as greedy, as determined to take the best for myself as my own father was, in the eyes of the servants, I've no doubt; why else, otherwise, would I wed Blanche Ingram, as everyone knows I mean to do? She is majestic certainly, but there are prettier and pleasanter about. I must be after her dowry, and the estate that marches with mine — and to Grace (and to my cousin, Mrs. Fairfax, though we never speak of what she must surely be aware of) I must seem a powerfully avaricious man, to take money from two brides in a row. So much for your dream of living as a stable lad, I can feel Grace Poole thinking, as if the drunken, illiterate woman could read my mind.

The table where my wife's keeper sits day and night is as it always is, that is, quite bare except for a bottle of porter and a glass. There is no other furniture, for Antoinette has in the past attempted to overthrow the press, where her old fine clothes, her red dress among them, hung; and Grace with my consent had this removed, along with the garments and their memories. There is one chair only, where Grace sits at the table, sleeping when she must, with her head on her hands. It takes me several seconds to recognize — in this mean, raftered room where straw is the sole floor covering and the view, as the attic windows are small and high, is of the narrow room behind, containing a single trundle bed — that the chair has been overturned and the bed (though I thought at first I must be mistaken, as there is no natural light to speak of in this cell) is without an occupant. I stare as stupidly at Grace Poole as she stares at me. It is impossible — yet it is what we have both most feared at Thornfield Hall. Antoinette — Bertha — my wife, has escaped, has disappeared into the house and is at large. Blanche Ingram, her mother, and her friends appear within the hour. And yet, as this foolish, evil-smelling woman and I both know, this was bound one day to occur, for all the pains we take to keep the door locked and the room padded to subdue the sound. The poor, demented creature dreamed only of escape. I cannot record my feelings on this here.

I descend the main staircase into the great hall with a heavy heart. (Grace, on coming to the first-floor landing, where are the master bedroom and the suites that will be Blanche and Lady Ingram's, has taken the back stairs, down to the servants' quarters. She fears for her job. I pay her double to keep quiet; now I shall have to triple her pay.) What would Céline do now? I ask myself; how would her philosophy have advised her in circumstances as unutterable as mine? "All men are born equal," said she as we lay in the quaint little house in Montparnasse I bought and furnished for her with such care — she telling all that she paid rent to a Monsieur Graff: she was ever the independent woman, Céline, and she liked to have her bread buttered on both sides. "Women have rights just as men do." And I think, what rights are these, then? Are not my chains, for all my lands and wealth, more oppressive than any poor man's? And I reach the Hall fuming at Céline, as I so often did when we were lovers. She would have insisted, very probably, that poor mad Bertha had the right to roam over my house as she would, disturbing the servants and the guests.

But Céline is not with me now, and she never will be again. Damn her, that even now my precious time is taken up in dreaming of a lost past, when a past more pernicious, more imminently damaging to my interests, walks murderously here. Curse the woman who preached freedom and brought me only servitude. For the last time — as I see Leah, guided by Grace Poole, scamper with a frightened face from the stone stairs to the lower floor into a corner of the Hall (what has Grace told her? forced finally to admit there is a lunatic about?) — for the last time I make the great effort of will to expunge La Varens forever from my mind. She is dead to me — dead, dead.

Then as I see Grace and Leah in fact go to the wide door, the door that stands between Thornfield Hall and the outside world, and a loud banging sounds against the studded nails and planks of old oak, I consign Céline forever to a well-merited oblivion. For this must be the Ingram party, come early, due to Blanche's eagerness to see the man she knows will propose before the week is out. Her mother, decked in pearls and diamonds, will shamelessly forecast the splendid gifts I shall promise to my bride. And they will bring with them a retinue — of young men as brainless as Céline (here I repeat, I will not think of her) assumes the rich, sporting Englishmen to be. "A *rosbif,* like you, Edouard!" her teasing voice sings in my ears. Her greatest contempt would be reserved for the young women, friends of my intended wife, and for their acceptance of their narrow lives. All these parasites will now descend on me, demanding hospitality, in one case devotion, even love. Céline, your spirit walks this house as my wife, my true wife. I cannot live without you. Go back, you said — but I will leave Thornfield Hall and come secretly to France, to live alone with memories of you, if these are all I am permitted to call my own. Let them arrest me and throw me into jail, may they send me to the guillotine for my crime. But I know, as Blanche Ingram approaches the heart of Thornfield Hall — my soul, the citadel of my youth, my future, and my past — that I cannot marry her and live an honest life.

The great door into the Hall swings open. John the footman appears, and Leah shrinks away into the shadows once more, while Grace, still seeking her quarry, I suppose, has vanished in the direction of the upper stories. Ah, I find myself thinking in the new, wild freedom my acceptance of the truth has at last brought to me, let the wretched specter of Antoinette appear now, just as the great families of Yorkshire come here for their hunting and cards and theatrical shows. Let them see the Creole from the islands where their fathers, like mine, traded in human cargo and paid with the evil profits for their snuffboxes, lace handkerchiefs, and the rest. Antoinette may be white — but she bears the marks of the slavery I imposed on her, and of my own cruel repudiation of her, too. Lords and ladies, do you wish to see your Blanche reduced to this?

The wide door, when it opens fully at last, does not reveal the neighboring gentry. A child stands on the threshold, dazed. She looks around her, then sees me and runs into my arms.

At first, I confess, I saw Céline there, a tiny woman, shrunk by magic to a fairy's size. The face — the smiling, dimpled face — the beauty, all miniature; and I thought I saw her fly to me, as she did in the circus in those far-off summer months. "This is a big house, monsieur," the child-woman cries out, as the household crowds around to stare at the apparition. And, as if to con-

firm my first fanciful idea, the little creature then asks if she would be allowed to
fly, in a *salle* as *grande* as this. "I have the
wings, Papa. Do you like to see?"

Four

Adèle

It was hotter, this past month, in Paris than had ever been recorded, so Félix said; Félix the copier of faces, complete with frowns and wrinkles. And in this weather, when faces ran and dripped with the heat, some fair monsters came up from the deeps of the chemical bath in his studio. But none with a physiognomy as vile, as clear a transcription of evil as Papa. Jenny Colon says I must now think of the man wanted by the French police, the man who never can return to the city where she claims poor Maman was held captive in her house in rue Vaugirard, by this name alone. "He is your father, Adèle. You must make your life with him, now Maman has gone. Be brave. He's not as bad as he looks."

I couldn't tell Jenny I knew more about the hideous stranger than she imagined. Her worship of Maman would falter, surely, if I described the evening, not so many months ago, when the milord wept on the balcony of the hotel he had furnished with such comfort for the woman he loved. She would find it hard to believe if I recounted the number of times Céline had led the lovers she swore she did not have past the chaise where I lay, feigning sleep, outside her bedroom door. And she would exorcise me forever from her life, I know, if I described to her that last, fateful morning: the mist that coiled along the banks of the Seine as the sun rose, the birds just rousing from night as we entered the Bois de Boulogne, the milord and his second, a valet named Edward, like his master, and — hidden from view in a pannier of bandages, fresh linen, and the rest — myself, Adèle Varens.

Jenny wouldn't believe me because everything has to be in black and white for her. Like Félix's studies of the famous and debauched — dear Gérard with his pet lobster, Gautier with his face like a map, all the arrondissements etched on his great forehead — Jenny is almost too "real" to be true. There is no mystery in her, and she expects none in her dealings with the world. In her eyes Maman is still perfect — and, most important, always at the mercy of men. Despite the fact that this victim, martyr to passion, deceived mistress of a murderer, has run off to Italy with the musician composer of the new opera at the Funambules, leaving her daughter an orphan, dependent on the generosity of Félix and the silent Pierrot. They have more to occupy them than an abandoned child — soon, as I know Jenny fears (for she cannot keep me; her tastes are not for domesticity and children), soon I shall be left to my own devices. In the street, in the mire and filth of Paris, you will find little Adèle, she who walked in rosy pink and blue behind her mother in the Luxembourg Gardens while Céline's companions, the painters and poets of Paris, spoke of their brilliant dreams of Utopia.

"I shall not write to your father," Jenny says as we set off for the place du Carrousel, where Nerval and his friends have a vast studio. "Better that we surprise him." Jenny, the blond chanteuse of *Piquillo*, will sing for them there, at the end of the Bal des Truands, the magnificent evening of bohemia for which they have long planned. "But you must leave tonight, before the feast is over. Courage, Adèle — your father will be delighted to welcome you to Thornfield Hall." But we both know, as we follow the sound of the cabaret orchestra smuggled through a hole in the fence in the Doyenné, that Jenny's decision to send me away from Paris in the wake of Maman's scandalous desertion is tantamount to a sentence of death. The man I must love with filial devotion is a Bluebeard, and his castle, I have little doubt, has locked and forbidden rooms where poor Maman, in the eyes of Jenny at least, would have languished if she had accepted his proposal to return with him to Thornfield as a bride.

For all that, I know that this monster of male selfishness and arrogance is not a murderer. Nor did he hold my mother prisoner in our house, as Jenny claims. He went to the Bois to fight a duel in defense of his honor (I, as I say, concealed in the basket with the fresh shirt and cravat and all the necessities for a wounded, bleeding duelist), and he returned to our house having killed a man. The vicomte it was who turned again, when Papa had winged him (he said the words quite lightly, I confess, like a hunter out shooting birds) when Maman took me there to meet her new, noble lover. He spoke like the huntsman who brings down a young partridge, and thinks nothing of it. But the vicomte it was who went against the rules of the duel. So the stern overseer in black said, who arranged the contest at first light in the Bois de Boulogne. The vicomte went against the rules of the game when he fired again, and Papa, a better shot by far, moved quickly and silently on that stretch of grass in the clearing in the wood, and on the grass still silver with the morning dew, he shot his rival dead.

As for Maman held hostage until Papa came back to her — why, he had no choice but to keep her in her bedroom under lock and key while he organized his escape from the gendarmes the vicomte's friends and supporters sent around (and there were many of them). *Pauvre* Papa — this is how I must think of him, now. *Pauvre* Papa: who loved me far better than Maman did, all along.

I speak of flying, for this summer, the summer of my exile from Paris and from all I loved best, was also the summer Jenny took me up in the circus, on wings fitted to my back with invisible wires, and I fluttered and dived high above the smiling crowd. How happy I was! She felt sorry for me, I suppose, for Maman had gone without a word of when or how I would ever see her again. And, in the same spirit, while Jenny taught me the divine gift of staying aloft — and instructed me, too, in the acting skills she said I would one day need — Félix made a point of taking me up in a hot-air balloon, the novelty of the season. We flew miles above all Paris and saw the Seine like a great green caterpillar as it crawled below, and Notre Dame so small I could have leaned down and taken it in my hand. "They have hot-air balloons at your Papa's," Félix said, trying to cheer me when we came down in a field farther out from the city than he had intended. But I knew, on the long journey back to Jenny's severe apartment where I stayed, that this was unlikely to be true.

La Cibot, the old witch, was right: it was the month of the crab, the dry, hot month of July that saw me going from Paris and through the dull fields of France, before crossing the gray sea. All this with a girl Jenny had appointed as my protector; but the girl stared out the window as I wept, and I had neither comforter nor friend. Only Maman's cashmere came with me. "He'll remember that even if he's forgotten you," said Jenny with one of her barking laughs as we set off. "He spent enough on it, God knows."

Yet I had something else with me also, a memento as the crone La Cibot termed it when pressing the great eye of glass into my hand after my last visit there. (I'd insisted, to Jenny: there might be a way of finding Maman, provided by the spirits with whom the hag was in communication. Maman, somewhere in Italy: but where?)

"You may need this, my child." La Cibot looked across at me, the table with its grubby cloth between us and Cleopatra the black hen asleep this time in a corner of the room, as if my presence without my mother and only with the unbelieving Jenny in tow was hardly worth waking for. "Look, do this — hold it up to the sun." And the fortune-teller went to the window to pull back the worn velvet curtain usually drawn against daylight and reason. "No, bring it down now, to that paper on the table — yes, that's right. *Ma petite* Adèle has quite a genius for the pyrotechnics, I can see." And La Cibot, for the first time, stood back and stared at me in admiration.

The fire began at first like the mark of a snail, a brownish smear across the lined paper where La Cibot jotted her expenses for the week. Then, as the trail began to bite, the words, the figures, and the penciled columns began to disappear. Flames half an inch high danced like the miniature *feux d'artifice* Félix liked to play with, a snake forming from a cigar, a clumsily built mouse, all on a plate in his studio. But this time I was the one who controlled the reality of fire, not the manufacturers of a childish toy. The flames began to grow higher, and then, as a rare gust of wind came in from the baking-hot day, they climbed higher still. The hen woke, I remember, as La Cibot, cursing, threw a basin of water over her own tabletop. "The fire likes you, Adèle," she said when she was done. "Respect it and it will be your servant forever. Use it with contempt and many will die."

I was afraid suddenly, in the room where the old witch summoned the dead and brought their messages to the unconsoled. I looked around for Jenny — but, just as I had feared, she was laughing at my fire-producing efforts and was as unimpressed as I had expected her to be. "Yes, give the child the magnifying glass by all means," said Maman's friend, pulling on her coat. "But I'm not paying extra, that's for sure. Besides, it won't be of much use where she's going" — and Jenny nodded at me sadly now. "There is no sun," she said with a horrible air of finality, "in *Angleterre*."

Now, with the disaffected girl snoring at my side, I can see how right Jenny was on that hot day that seems now to be no more than a distant dream. The fields are dead-looking, drenched under the recent rain bursts, and the sky is heavily wrapped in cloud. With each mile the air grows darker, making me believe that the English live in a permanent night. The horses standing by the clogged streams look dispiritedly up at us. This cannot be half of me, I think; I do not belong in this landscape. But there is no one to whom I can confide the thought. Silence as oppressive as the gloom comes down on me, as we turn up a long drive with a line of dripping trees on either side. "I refuse to live here" — this I say aloud, as the driver turns and points out a tall house, gray as an executioner's block, with battlements like sharp blades rearing into the sky. "This is the place I must run from — to Italy, to the blue sea and Maman, to love."

But if I arrive at Thornfield Hall knowing myself a stranger here, the man I must call Papa clearly thinks otherwise. As he comes to catch me in his arms, I make a show of little-girl affection and fly to him, babbling of the circus wings I have brought along with me, a performer to the last. As I do so, another batch of visitors arrives at the great house. I do not know yet how rare the arrival of company is here at

Thornfield. "Ah, Blanche," says Papa to a tall, dark young woman as she comes into the Hall. She looks around, I see, as if she owns it. Papa sets me down on a marble floor that is checkered like a chessboard and says to the visitors, with a sarcastic growl I recognize too well, "You have chosen the hour of your coming most carefully."

"Why? Who is this?" demands the tall, stately lady as she strides over the cold marble and tries to avoid me in her greeting of the host.

"Oh, it's no one," Papa says, laughing, while a woman with breath that stinks of an alcohol we do not have in France comes forward to lead me away to the nursery and an early bed. "It's my little French bastard, if you want to know. Adèle Varens."

It is cold here, as cold as Jenny said it would be. *La vieille dame,* Madame Fairfax, tells me there is a Jack Frost who comes each night to write on the windowpane of my room — and it is true his scribbles are there when I wake, as hard to decipher as the smiles and frowns of the man I am told by Jenny to call Papa, but who wishes none of that word from me. I am closer to Monsieur Frost, I think sometimes, as I sit alone in the room where one darkness succeeds another — the brown twilight hour, then the blackness of night, followed only by a gray that lies like the pelt of a dead animal over field and meadow and lea — I am closer to this invisible writer of cold than I am to the man who has told his friends from the great world outside of his rescue of a pitiful bastard from the Paris gutter.

Seven weeks have passed — I count them on the tassel from the *robe de chambre* that was once my mother's, the only memento I have of the days in rue Vaugirard. The rosy cotton, padded Turkish style to keep Maman snug in her long mornings sipping coffee or rehearsing her lines carries still the faint musk or jasmine of her scent — but I must not think of her, so Jenny says; and Madame Fairfax cannot think of her at all, for she has no knowledge of the most beautiful woman, the most celebrated actress in all Paris. "I shall be with you soon, *ma chérie*," Maman says to me in my daydreams by the dark window where Jack's white pen lingers until late on the casement. "Don't forget how much I love you." And although I have no memory of my mother's saying those words to me, I feel the love that Nadar says I hide too much, feel it come to my cheeks and turn them pink and glowing. I shall show everyone here what I am capable of . . . this child with her French airs no one likes or understands. I shall earn the love of Papa and I must try — however hard this may prove to be — to unlearn the way the mimes and actors show themselves to the world, for it is not popular here.

"My dear, I have visited the theater once, in Bradford," says the old lady when I press her for some reminiscence that lies outside the fortress where I am imprisoned, Thornfield Hall. "But I recall little other than a sad love scene: lovers who were not permitted to meet — something of the kind. There wasn't a dry eye in the house, if I look back on it." And then the housekeeper, usually so bustling and occupied, so quick to reprimand Leah or send me shooting to my room for slippers to keep my toes from turning to pillars of ice, falls silent, and I feel guilt at her sadness, though she will never tell me why I should. Sometimes, I admit, I misbehave simply to gain the attention of this cousin of Papa (so is she my cousin also? I hardly think she desires me as kin), and I run all over this house where each story, in the frightful gloom, appears to belong belowstairs. "The great Thornfield Hall," I wrote to Jenny in my first week here — but six more weeks have passed, and she still has not replied to me — "is no more than three basements, one on top of the other." Little did I know then that one further subterranean level existed, high above the sad, tenebrous room I have been allotted, as neither gentry nor servant class. How unaware I was, of a hell plucked from the nether regions and set up under the battlements in the unrelenting whiteness of the winter sky. For me, at first, the sense of a vertigo, almost an indifference as to which way to go when meeting stairs that soar or plummet to floors nearer or farther from the man I must woo, must love — my Papa who does not yet understand me — reflected merely my own uncertainty of my status in this odd, frozen household. Are maids to look up or down at me? Does Madame Fairfax's occasional gentleness reveal a secret knowledge of all the treats Papa has in store for me, once his grand guests have departed, once — even though I do not like to think of it — his engagement to Mademoiselle Ingram is announced? Will the governess I am told will come any day now to instruct me in the manners of a young English lady demonstrate to Mademoiselle Blanche the superior nature and breeding of her charge? Or shall I be ignored forever? I had no direction; I could be led or left to my own devices, as people chose.

But now I have no more impatience for the coming of the governess. For, in the most unlikely of places, I have found a friend. It happened in this way. A day of blustery autumn squalls had kept the house filled and the park and gardens empty at Thornfield: Mademoiselle Blanche, in all her finery, had no desire to step into puddles or subject her coiffure to the high winds that raced across the moor and stripped leaves from the trees in Papa's proud avenue; and her mother, Lady Ingram, along with the other guests, had settled in the red and white drawing room, a room I was not allowed on pain of death to enter. "Do remove the brat from here," I heard Miss Blanche cry out on those occasions when I persuaded Leah to dress me up in the rose organdy Papa had brought me back from Paris, a sure tribute to his undying love for Maman and for their darling, *petite* Adèle. "The child gets on my nerves" — these were the words she invariably used; but when I said to La Fairfax that I had no wish for this monster as my step*maman*, the housekeeper would smooth her apron and look away, muttering that there would be no step*maman* in sight, the way things were at Thornfield Hall; and as I had no intimation of the good woman's meaning, the subject of the approaching nuptials of Monsieur Rochester would be abandoned yet again. So I felt myself neither welcomed nor dismissed when I entered the red and white drawing room in my party frock; for, after all, Mademoiselle Ingram had less right than I to be there, for all her languid occupation of the big sofa right under the window. Was I not the daughter of the house? And did it not seem increasingly unlikely that Blanche would reign as chatelaine? Yet, as so often in this puzzling *maison de campagne*, which is neither castle nor manor house, I saw Monsieur Rochester obey Miss Blanche as if she were indeed his chosen bride; and he would pick me up and forcibly throw me into the hall, as if I were no more than an unwanted puppy. It is true to say that until I made my new friend here, I had as little notion of my place as the weathervane high on Papa's battlements, turning and turning in the wind.

On this particular day, as I say, the house was filled to overflowing with people who had as little capacity for amusing themselves as sheep shut up in a pen. When I considered the *jeux de cartes,* the charades, and the operettas Maman and Jenny would stage on rainy Sundays as the dull gentlemen and their wives knelt at prayer in the church of Saint-Germain en Laye, or as the great chimes of Notre Dame sounded out across the city, bidding clowns and actors, gamblers and dancers to abandon their frivolity and invest in the life after death — when I thought of all the amusements we contrived, I felt true pity for these *anglais* and their inability to do more than stuff down *le rosbif* at luncheon and yawn all day as the rain came down outside. I had learned to occupy, even to fascinate, myself by exploring the ancestral home of *mon cher* Papa, at those times when Yorkshire threatened to engulf us with its gloom and downpours. For me, the great hall with its oak staircase was as full of excitement and promise as a child's toy theater (such as Papa had bought me, from a rare visit to London, red cardboard, gold paper proscenium, and all). Which door would I enter, from that square hall that was so forbidding to enter from outside that Madame Fairfax said she could swear the ghost of old *Grandmère* Rochester lingered there, beneath her portrait in the rope of cold pearls? (For I was not afraid: if this is my home, I shall occupy it as my ancestors have done.) Which dark, somber day will have me try the door that leads upward, to the servants' staircase I have seen a strange woman come down — followed by Grace, she who fills her tankard on the half hour while Madame Fairfax clucks her tongue and who comes to pull the stranger back up again, with as little courtesy as Papa and Mademoiselle Ingram practice on me? It was that day, just less than a week ago and at the time of the Ingram stay here at Thornfield Hall, that I showed those who suffered from ennui how to find novelty and pleasure, at even the saddest and drabbest of times.

Mademoiselle — she who dreams she will be the fiancée of the squire — is in one of her moods today. La Fairfax teaches me that "squire" is the word that describes Papa, but I do not like it: Papa is a milord, as Maman and Jenny both knew, for all their impatience with his rude and rough ways. A squire is a countryman, a man who lives with his pigs and cows, or so it sounds to me, and Papa travels the world. The grand tour has opened before him, and he has returned with marble statues and pictures as wide and long as colonnaded streets and mountain ranges: Europe has offered its treasures to Papa. Mademoiselle, as I say, is in a bad mood and has just had the temerity and ill breeding to eject me once more from the drawing room, so I find myself, on this cold and overcast day, alone and forgotten in the square hall. Blanche will never be Madame Rochester, that is certain; and just as I stand shivering in the white silk mousseline with the cherries and rosebuds appliquéd on the hem and attempt to imagine a good prank to play on the haughty beauty, the door that leads to the servants' staircase opens, and a flash of a dirty petticoat shows, before its owner stumps out into the hall, empty tankard in hand. Grace — for it is she — ignores me as she makes for the kitchen, though why she hasn't gone straight down to take her supply from the cellars I don't know. At the same time the door from the billiard room bursts open and the rest of the Ingram party comes out, bloated and yawning as usual, Grace disappearing from sight as they emerge.

This is my chance to bring some life and

laughter to the wretched *anglais*. Doesn't Papa remember, when we used to play *cache-cache* at the house where Maman lived and she would sometimes allow him to climb right up into her bedroom, when we all played the game? Won't Papa follow, when he hears me cry, as La Fairfax had told me were the words, "Hide and seek! Catch me if you can!"

Papa did not come from the red and white drawing room, where he sat with a mournful expression, listening to Blanche at her interminable airs on the piano. But the rest of the party did: within one minute, or so it seemed, a whole herd of young men and silly girls in dresses with the puffed sleeves we have so long ago discarded in Paris are chasing me up the narrow servants' staircase to the top of the house. And I am too breathless — too excited and even afraid — to stop and look back and arrest them as they rush upward. For I, too, am ignorant of what lies here, in the domain guarded by Grace and never referred to by Madame Fairfax, as if a whole story of Thornfield Hall simply, and just because she had decided thus, had ceased to exist. If I am to hide, what and whom is it they must seek? For I hear the screams of excitement, that I lead them to

the ghost — "Oh, it's Edward's grandmother, the housekeeper told me so" — as
I mount, and emerge at last onto a landing
that even I, in all my explorations of the
Hall, have never seen.

It is dark up here, the ceilings are low,
and it is some time before I see the
landing, which, unlike the rooms in this
fine house, is carpeted in something hard
— like matting put down for beasts, I
cannot stop myself from thinking; this
tough straw is not for the likes of Mademoiselle Ingram and her friends. Light
comes in from mansard windows — such
as Nadar worked by, poor Nadar who lived
for the good strong light of day. Pictures,
some so tall they must have been sent up
here when they were no longer à la mode
— some of ladies and gentlemen, all sad
and somber as this house lost in the dark
moors would make them — hang un-
observed on the sloping walls; and even as
I run past, I see the features of Monsieur
de Rochester (as I secretly know him, for
Papa is as noble as Maman's vicomte)
there, though not my own, for all I try to
grimace into the frames.

Why has it become so silent? The footsteps of the young men and the scurrying
girls are muffled now, and I realize they

have run off in the opposite direction, drawn, I suppose, by the fact that the passage opens out there, promising further rooms and antique furniture to exclaim over: it is possible to hear, in the distance, one of Mademoiselle Blanche's chosen confidantes cry out in delight over a sewing basket set in a marquetry table, a rubbishy thing poor Irène at home would have discarded long ago. Then the troupe meets someone — Grace perhaps, on her way back up the stairs with her jug of porter — and a silence falls, this time broken only by murmurs of apology: Madame Fairfax, maybe, coming into the terrain she will never mention, to throw out those who have no right to go in search of the Thornfield Hall ghost. I stop and find that my head touches the ceiling above me, and the passage has narrowed before turning to yet another flight of steps, these smaller still than those I have climbed to the landing behind me. Shall I return and explain to the good housekeeper that we play *cache-cache*, the game I tried to describe to her, when we sit by the fire in the evenings and Madame Fairfax says the governess will be here soon and I shall have more to occupy me than the recounting of my past life to an old woman who falls asleep? Am I to go in search of those English who hunt and cry "Tally ho!" when they are out in the field but look on me as invisible as a mouse? I am free now; I have no need to hide when no one comes to seek. And so it is that I fit my foot — small even for my age and height, as Jenny has informed me with one of her rare smiles — I place my foot on the stair and see that it covers the tread entirely, as if this way upward could be taken by none other than Adèle Varens, by *une petite fille,* by the child for whom it was fashioned — for so, as I climb on and on, this strange staircase seem to me to be.

After several twists and turns — and with any sound of Madame Fairfax or the retreating party entirely subdued and gone — I see a light ahead of me on the stairs and, as I turn the last, almost impossibly squeezed corner, a large window can be seen to shed its light on wall and staircase. The window is ajar, and the sill is easy — or easier — to step onto than the next, vertiginous step. Accordingly, as if I had known all along I must walk out onto the forbidden roof of Papa's house, I do so. The leads feel soft, as if melted by a sun seldom known to Thornfield; and they are bound, or confined, by lengths of piping, where I take care to walk, for fear of stumbling on the uneven flat surface. At first, anxious to preserve my balance, I do not look up. I know that a magnificent view will be my reward when I do, but the mock cannons, roughly hewn from gray stone, are all I permit myself in the early stages of my illicit visit to the roof. What if I were to fall? I can't help thinking of the trouble that would come to Madame Fairfax, of whom I have become fond, in the absence of anyone else with whom to exchange affectionate gestures. I must take great care not to go tumbling down to the ground.

When at last I do look up, I see her. The purplish haze of heather on the moors, fading in the fast-encroaching winter but strong enough in color still to lend the air of an ocean painted by one who dreamed of foreign seas, stretches out behind her in the clear air. The thorn trees, parterres, fine vegetable gardens, and outbuildings of Thornfield Hall lie as neat as a child's toy on the land claimed from the wildness of the moors. The ornamental lake glitters like a teardrop put there by one of Maman's *amis* in Paris, on the waxen cheek of my favorite *poupée*, Christine. All is artificial, removed, minute — with the exception of the woman who stands facing me now, not six inches from the parapet. She is haggard, her black hair tumbles down her back, and she holds her arms out to me. She alone, on these battlements of Papa's where the guns cannot fire and the turrets, with their pepperpot hats, could sustain neither siege nor attack, is real. Behind her, like a backdrop in the Funambules, hangs the likeness of the landscape surrounding and enclosing Thornfield Hall. The woman, with faltering steps, approaches me. *"Mon doudou,"* she says, and her voice is thick, thicker than the voice of Grace when she has been at her porter and I'm hurried away from her, on the stairs. *"Viens,"* the strange woman says. Her accent places her somewhere in my memory, but I cannot for now think just where. She is French — that is all I know now — she is French, and she is my new friend, brought to me here on the roof of Thornfield Hall.

I soon learned how to keep the secret of the lady who lives out on the parapet and battlements of the house Jenny says I must think of as my home — but I cannot, I cannot. The *étrangère* (for I can see that poor Antoinette, as she tells me I can call her, is as much a stranger in this place as I am) has found a little *maison* all her own, in the turret, and here she has placed a quilt that is the color of the exotic flowers Maman preserved and brought back with her from the time she went to dance in Martinique, far, far away across the sea. My friend sleeps when the sun goes down, and I bring her food, smuggled up from the plain, horrible meals Leah takes up twice a day to the schoolroom. Leah is accustomed to seeing my plate go back still piled with the stews and overboiled legumes of this sad country, and I have had to pretend to an appetite I never had before. But it is worth the stories I must make up. Madame Fairfax also must believe I wish for time to study my English verbs, in preparation for the new governess, though she has come to see me, I know, as I really am, a child in need of company, a budding actress who desires an audience for the canzonets and lovesick ballads she was taught to sing at her mother's knee.

All this is worth the trouble. Antoinette is not like the English ladies: Blanche with her hauteur that chills me to the bone, even Madame F who looks right through me sometimes when I prattle on. Antoinette understands the colors, the muslins, silks, and satins I bring in, scraps from dresses now outgrown but kept — kept like the memories of Maman they bring each time I lift them from the drawer, in the tissue paper the maid Sophie provides for them. Antoinette, who speaks on occasion in a tongue I cannot understand — but then she laughs and returns to French or English; she says her patois is from an island where she will take me one day, a Windward island, as she calls it, where she was happy once — Antoinette will play with me and hold me close as if we had known each other in a time before either of us was brought here to the cold of Thornfield Hall. *"Chérie, doudou,"* she whispers to me, and I smell the firewater on her breath. And — when she thinks we are about to be disturbed at our games high on the roof — *"Qui est là? Qui est là?"* she calls out, which reminds me so strongly of our parrot in the rue Vaugirard, Monsieur Punch, that I place them in my mind in the same landscape, where the hot-colored flowers Antoinette loves bloom all year long and the moths are as large as Papa's silk handkerchiefs.

I will never know how it took so long for Grace Poole to discover us in our hideaway on the roof. Because it was raining, perhaps, and we had stepped across the sill (this was the first time for my new friend; she had as great a dislike for the indoors at Thornfield Hall as I had for the gray, sodden walks Madame F made me take "for my health" — and many more to come, she promises me, when this governess arrives: how I hate "Mademoiselle" already, with her brown brogues and her stick that pokes into the foliage of the hedges we go past and then pass again on our dreary excursions. Adèle will find plenty of headaches to keep her away from the schoolroom; then I'll hide and run back to the turret house of *ma chère* Antoinette, that's for certain).

But Antoinette hated one thing more than any other, and that was the very notion of being locked in somewhere, as I was to learn. For I had found a low door, several twisting stairs down from the big window that leads out onto the roof. The door was square, and even for me it was necessary to bend almost in two to push it open and go in; also there was a shelf that must be mounted before crawling through the aperture into the hidden room.

Antoinette refused at first to step from the freedom of the roof back into the house. But when I told her what I saw in this boxroom — for this, I suppose, is what it was: a repository of all the old, unwanted, and unremembered childhoods of the girls and women of the *famille* Rochester — my new friend was no longer able to resist coming to join me. She was tall, and it was hard at first for her to double up (she let out a laugh when she came to kneel on the shelf by the low door that would have made me afraid of her if I had not known her to be gentle and loving at all times), but once she was through and down with me on the wooden planks, I knew I had never seen her so happy or so taken with what lay before her.

The room was higher than the door, but not by much. I could walk upright; Antoinette could not. Yet the fact of having to stoop in this way drew her attention to the floor of glass in the farthest part of the room, and, skirting a colony of drowsy bees on the way there (I had stopped to pull their wax houses apart in the search of honey), I followed her as she stood goggling at the room that lay beneath us in the highest attic of Thornfield Hall.

A bathroom was visible through the grime of the glass tiles, these clearly unwashed since their incorporation into this house built by Mr. Rochester's grandfather

— or so Madame Fairfax had attempted to instruct me, with the idea that I should show proper reverence for the château to which I had been brought as a destitute orphan. A bath, long and greenish in color; a commode of wood with a cane back to the seat, giving the contraption an air of an African throne — as I thought, at least, remembering the plates in the books of native tribes Nadar had shown me, in the room where he invented faces, both sad and humorous. A basin, a washstand, two pictures (but the light was too dim to make these out; they seemed to portray lakes and moors and be colored with the false purples bad painters use to portray the landscape of this district). And in the bath, motionless and pale, naked as the day he was born, none other than Monsieur Rochester, the milord and proprietor of all he surveys at Thornfield. Antoinette, seeing him first, gave out a great yell. Monsieur Rochester looked up, frowning, and then sat upright in the bath. Antoinette, falling backward on a painted rocking horse, grasped its mane, made of a molting wire wool, and proceeded to mutter strange words into the black and white wooden ear, complete with jingle bells, which her powerful arms pulled toward her. I in turn ran to my new friend's side and buried my head in her skirts. I had no idea then, of any connection between the man Jenny says I must know as Papa and the woman from the spice islands who sings to me as a Creole maid of Maman's once did, songs my new playmate says come from an old woman who loved her, Christophine. I shut my eyes and feel the heaving, sobbing sound Antoinette makes when her laughter turns to wild grief. The rocking horse shakes its head, and the little silver bells ring out. We are away from the glass part of the boxroom floor by now, and as we stumble away we fall against two basketwork saddles, these fashioned for children no more than four years old, and I see perched in them two tiny figures, the dead twin sisters Madame F had told me of, the aunts of Monsieur Rochester. I scream . . . and I scream again. And as the low door from the stairs opens and Grace scrambles in with Madame F close behind her, I leave poor Antoinette lying like a corpse on the floor as I rush into the housekeeper's arms.

Five

Edward

I am in danger of losing my marriage, my hopes for the future, everything. If there is a spirit haunting this house, it belongs to the child sent by the devil to put me in my mind of my past errors and sins; it is the spirit of chaos and destruction, learned at its mother's knee, the spirit of revolution and subversion, the end of the order established here since time immemorial, commemorated and celebrated on the tablets in the ancient church of Thornfield, revered and respected throughout the countryside.

God (and he is banished also, by the fire of disobedience and rebellion that sweeps through the once-orderly corridors of this great house) — God alone knows whether the child is mine (though I do observe, I freely confess, some of the traits in my own nature that I have prayed to the deity to assist in erasing: namely, pride, arrogance, and a desire to keep what is closest to the heart concealed). The child's wickedness

may be the natural and inevitable consequences of an upbringing that can barely
be described as such: a mother more absent than lovingly present; a camaraderie
of acrobats and atheists with no more wish
to reach the gates of heaven than the
highest wire in the circus tent can provide;
and, to underline the importance of a
guiding spirit in matters of the affections, a
sapphic blackmailer such as the woman
who signs herself "Jenny" in her imperti-
nence, when she writes to demand further
money from me. No, to add these charac-
teristics to those of the child's own dear
mother — namely cunning, deceit, and a
huge measure of vanity and self-regard —
there is little surprise in the discovery that
Adèle Varens, at eight years old, is already
wedded to the devil and beyond conver-
sion or repair. Whether she is my child or
not, her home is not here among these
gentle hills and moors, but in the infernal
regions. She shall leave Thornfield at the
earliest opportunity: already my marriage
to Miss Ingram is compromised, my fortune halved by my reluctance to propose a
settlement in the course of their last visit.
Nor was it ever possible to find a time to
make the proposal of matrimony I had
fully intended. The brat flew in, a malign

sprite, on the very day my estates were due to grow in revenue and magnificence. My mother's diamonds lie untouched in their chest here in my library — and it grieves me to add that I shall now need to lock them away, while this thieving Jacobin guttersnipe is about. Miss Ingram has gone off discontented, and Lady Ingram spoke of insult as I bade her farewell at the door of the Hall. To cap it all, one of the young blades of the party hinted that he had had designs on the lovely Blanche for some years now and that he had held off in deference to the master of Thornfield. Another, smirking insufferably, muttered something to the effect that "Mr. Rochester's fortune is but a third of what it is said to be," and I discovered, only this morning, that papers of mine are vanished from the strongbox here — the very same box where the jewels intended for my bride languish unoffered to her. Blanche saw to it that I must lay all this misfortune at the door of the devil's daughter. Adèle must go; in the grime of Paris streets I have no doubt she will have the wits to survive; and should she fall by the wayside, let her do so before the future of this great estate is further threatened by the actions of one whom the French libertarians would proclaim as heir, for all she is female and born illegitimate, of Thornfield and its outlying lands. Adèle shall never prove me to be her father: if I lose all I have in doing so, I shall contest the accusation of paternity of Céline's offspring to the end of my days.

I pick up my handbell; the dog, Pilot, stirs by the fire at the familiar ring, but no one comes. I rise, my impatience and wrath mounting as they do daily at these evidences of indifference to my wishes on the part of the staff of Thornfield Hall. I am answered nowhere now, when I call. I am further subjected to the indignity of finding myself goggled at in the bath from the attic above, by the little brat. Worse, I could swear that the bloated features of my wife, Bertha — on that day caught and returned to her cell — stared down at me, she kneeling beside the child. However many the tricks the little fiend decides to play on me, nothing shall take Edward Fairfax Rochester from his rightful occupancy of the house constructed by his ancestors.

I pick up the bell again, but as its chime rings out, the door opens and a small figure comes quietly in. It stands there, this elf in a gray, modest costume, its eyes lowered as befits one in the presence of the master of the greatest estate in Yorkshire. "Well, Jane," say I — for I have come to find a soothing quality in this young woman, the newly arrived governess of Céline's diabolical daughter. "Is there no servant to answer my command? Did you come from kindness, to minister to my needs?"

"No, sir." Miss Eyre looks up at me, but I see she is shy and does not wish to meet my gaze.

"What then?" I glance down at the antique rings and pendants in the box at my feet. They are still mine; they do not yet adorn the snowy bosom of Miss Ingram. And for a moment — but I am mad indeed; my fancies and illusions of past days are all the fault of the malevolent spirit unleashed on this house by the unbaptized child — for a moment I am inclined to walk over to "Miss Aire," as the little goblin addresses her, and fasten them at her slender neck. "How do you like diamonds, Jane?" I cannot prevent myself from blurting out nonetheless, and I hold up a strand of the magic stones in their old silver settings, a ray of sun coming in the window and turning them to a cascade of sparkling stones.

"I have not given thought as to whether I

have a liking for them or not," replies Miss Eyre — as she is rightly called, a name as plain as she herself. "I came to say, sir, that Adèle needs shoes for country walking. She has brought only dancing shoes or satin slippers, and these are, naturally, unsuitable for the lanes here."

Suitable for walking away from Thornfield forever, I thought, but for one reason or another I did not voice my opinion of the governess's request. "Very well," I said, and I heard myself growl most uncharitably as I replied. Yet I had confided in this young woman, this Jane from nowhere, only last evening in the garden, when I had told her of Adèle's origins — and then of my past passion and my jealousy for the child's mother, the actress Céline Varens. "You don't hold it against me, do you, Jane?" said I as she came up to my proffered hand and took the note I had scribbled for Cousin Fairfax, that she instruct the cobbler at Whitfield to fashion a pair of stout shoes for the governess's young charge. "You don't think the less of me, for describing to you last night the feelings of the human heart?"

"You said yourself, sir," responded Jane Eyre, retreating as fast as her natural dignity and modesty would permit her, and addressing me only when she had reached the door, "you said I should know such passions when I was older, sir, and you have been kind in warning me."

With this ambiguous statement the small figure left the room. I stood on awhile, still holding a strand of diamonds and looking all the more foolish for it, I daresay. And I reminded myself that Bertha, my wife, must never be permitted to escape again, from the cell I had constructed for her. I must be safe in the knowledge that the wretch is under lock and key, before Blanche Ingram comes here again. Before the hunting season is out, I will fasten these stones under the heiress's great mane of dark hair. And by then Adèle Varens will have left Yorkshire — and England — forever.

Then it occurs to me that without the child here there will be no need for a governess at Thornfield Hall. "A good economy," I say aloud; but I know, if only as faintly as a cloud that passes over the moon and then wanders on into the night sky, that this economy would not do good for me after all. I need the quiet presence of Miss Eyre at Thornfield Hall — why, damn it, I must admit I do.

Six

Adèle

I detest the creature Papa has ordered from a seminary to come here as my *gouvernante*. This "Miss Aire" governs nobody, with her independent views, however: she appears instead to love the authority Maman and Jenny showed me how to hate. "Yes, sir. No, sir," says the disagreeable little thing, when Monsieur Rochester invites us for such a brief minute to sit with him in the library. And he smiles at her in return! "Yes, sir," when he orders her to take me off to bed. Yet this man I first knew as Bluebeard has been kinder to me, of late — when he is not in one of his rages, *c'est à dire* — than in the days after the visit of Mademoiselle Blanche, when I was the *raison* for everything that went wrong in the running of the house. Perhaps he compares Miss Eyre, as I must learn to call her name, with the child he does on occasion accept as his daughter with the great Céline Varens. Little wonder he smiles fondly at me, as I run with the battledore and shuttlecock Leah is permitted to play with me on the long lawn at Thornfield Hall. Papa sees the results of his noblesse and Maman's talents, combined in me. In Jane he sees only the persistent banality of her mind and an adherence to rules and regulations doubtless instilled at the seminary. Jane can never become a grande dame — whereas I have a future without bounds that lies for me just over the horizon. I have only the lack of *ma chère mère* to trouble me; but as I become the famous actress she always predicted I would be, we shall all be one happy family together: Papa, Maman, and Adèle. And definitely no Jane Eyre!

For the time, I contain my rage and misery as best I can. As I sit in the schoolroom and go through the English verbs and the sums the young woman with the pale, closed-in face makes me do, I nurse my secret in silence. I smile to myself, that the meek governess who has nevertheless a fine picture of her own way of doing things, a self-satisfaction that would have had Jenny Colon reaching for the whip, has no idea of the existence of my new friend high in the attic of this house. Yes, *ma pauvre amie* was captured by Madame F and Grace Poole and placed in her cell, behind a door that could never be stormed, even stronger than the Bastille. I can time my visits to within one minute by now. When Grace is down at the cellars or the kitchen, to fill up her tankard of porter, she leaves the inner door unlocked, and I can go in to embrace my friend and chatter in the language that comes from the rain forests where Gérard, Maman's friend, found and captured our parrot, Monsieur Punch.

Once, it is true, I very nearly gave away my secret — and it was indeed when the vexed subject of the revolution in France had to be raised, for Miss Eyre guided me through the kings and queens of England and France and arrived at our last king with, so I considered, a smile of sympathy for the *monstre* on her face. "Louis?" said she. "You have remembered the Bourbon and the Orléans families, Adèle. But you have not given me the names of the guillotined monarch and his consort."

"Citizen Capet," I replied crossly.

"And his queen, who knew such unhappiness and lost her son the dauphin in the prison to which they were both confined for many months," pressed the dull little Puritan, Miss Eyre. (But she is at heart a monarchist; of this I am quite sure.)

"Antoinette," I said; and as I spoke the

name of my friend, I cried aloud at the injustice of those at Thornfield Hall: namely Grace Poole and Papa, who want no one to know of the woman they keep shut up there, without sunlight or chance of escape. *Why* she is there I have never asked — and I began to speak violently and eagerly of my friend before I remembered that Miss Eyre will go straight to Papa if I reveal my secret, and he will be angry with me again. *"Ce n'est rien,"* I said when I had recovered myself and Miss Eyre had announced our lesson over, thus giving me an extra ten minutes in which to play with poor Antoinette. "I wept for the queen of France, the massacred innocent," I said. For I had seen a miniature, very sentimentally executed, of the late Marie Antoinette, thus labeled and displayed on a table at the house of a woman who paid Jenny to take her riding on horseback in the Bois de Boulogne. "My heart bleeds for her," I went on, deceiving my interlocutor, as I knew I should. "You are tired today," said Miss Eyre — and when she is kind, I must harden my heart against her, for Maman is the only one I love. "Go and run in the garden awhile. The rain is holding off."

I said I would do the bidding of Miss

Eyre. But I ran up the stairs and then through the door behind the tapestry where visitors to the Hall say they sometimes see a ghost — although, *naturellement*, I know the identity of this "ghost" — and up again to the low rafters of the third story. I have a treat for my Antoinette in store: I have found the chest with all the dresses Grace hid from her, the red dress especially, of which the sad *prisonnière* speaks so often and with such passion. "We'll play weddings, *doudou* — you shall be my husband and I your Antoinette."

But when I arrive at the bare room that Grace should, by all rights, have left at this hour in order to replenish her jug with ale or porter, I find that the steel door to the inner cell is locked. I knock on it as hard as I dare, but no answer comes.

Perhaps because I have been at my lessons with Jane, I think when I stand by the door of a steel blade descending, slicing through the neck of a woman who is not the queen of France but who is instead my Antoinette. Then I see what appears at first to be a scrap of waste paper on the floor, near the door that separates *la folle* from those who have the good fortune to run free at Thornfield Hall. I go to pick it up. A wedding bouquet . . . even in its faded and derelict state I can see that it consisted once of flowers and had a satin ribbon tied around the dried and emaciated stalks. But the flowers are not rosebuds or *muguets,* lilies of the valley, as would befit a bridal banquet in France. These are tropical blooms — tall, spiked — like dying moths they droop in extinct oranges and indigo blues. And I remember Antoinette as she told me of the great shoots of color that blossom all year long, the hibiscus and frangipani and orchids that grew on the island where she once was happy. This was her wedding bouquet, all those years ago. What happened to her after this?

Autumn has come. The days pass, and the hedges that mark out the lanes to Millcote and Whitcross begin to turn from green to copper, while the tall trees that line the avenue — the trees I first saw when I came to Thornfield and thought them weeping, so endless were the raindrops that pattered from them onto the road — shed their leaves in the strong autumn winds blowing in from the moors.

The days pass, but there is still neither sign nor sound anywhere in the house of the strange woman I made my friend.

Grace I cannot ask directions on the whereabouts of her secret prisoner — for Antoinette was indeed a secret for both of us, but one we could not share. Leah — who has fallen in love with Jack the stable lad and places little *cadeaux,* or notes that contain no more than a heart pierced by an arrow, on scraps purloined from the library wastebasket and placed in a hole in a tree in the garden — looks mysterious if I hint that the upper house is quieter now than it used to be, or even if I demand outright to know why Grace Poole stays in that room of hers when it appears she now has no one to converse with or take her orders. "No," Leah says as we walk down the lime walk and stand a moment by the clump of trees known as the Four Ashes, just beyond the stable walls. "No, there is nothing changed here at the Hall." And she puts her hand deep into a cleft in the tree and pulls out a packet, small and bulging with Jack's latest gift: today a pebble, fished from the stream up by Whitfield Height, where the pools lie deep and clear, the rough brown stone containing a glint of river gold that runs in a vein across the surface. The stone has been pierced — with a chisel, very probably — for the hole is barely wide enough to contain a slender chain, this of the cheapest materials — or so my Parisian eyes, trained in all manner of jewelry from scrutinizing Maman's *bijouterie,* immediately tell me. Leah is pleased with today's offering, however, and slips the stone around her neck; and I reflect, as some of the other servants emerge from the back door of the house — John the footman going into the stables with a purposeful air (Monsieur Rochester has sent him with instructions to have his horse ready, perhaps; he always issues his commands at the very last minute and then is impatient when things do not happen all at once) — I reflect that my time for grilling Leah on the subject of the disappeared Antoinette has slipped away again.

But thinking of Maman's jewels and then of the last trace of my poor friend, she who lived on the roof happy as a bird, snug at night in her little pepperpot house, has led me to think with even greater concentration of the future here at Thornfield Hall. And as I try to envisage this future, I also find myself wondering at the changes that have overtaken me in the past months, some so alarming, I confess, that I wish for Jenny, stern though she may be, as a guide to my new, different state. For how can I explain the dreaminess that seizes me, even on the clearest day Yorkshire can provide, and the sense that I see what is not there, as if this old house, to which I have become so accustomed, has given birth to a new family of ghosts? I feel myself, quite literally, without balance or ballast on the days when this affliction descends — the very trees in the avenue at Thornfield change color, as if precipitated into a false autumn, and the clouds, packed with the usual rain, dance in the strangest shapes across the sky. Is all this due to my fears for the future — the future, that is to say, when Papa and Maman are married at last and we are all happy together, happy, as the fairy tales have it, as the day is long? How can I arrange it, that what is right shall take place — after all the crimes people say Papa committed, and some of them a result, as I so well know, of my mother's own wrongdoing, her luring of the man she truly loves into killing the vicomte. As a result of the terrible jealousy she produced in *mon pauvre* Papa, the vicomte is dead and Monsieur Rochester can no longer return to France. How, then, can I bring them together? And yet now, as I stand thinking under the Four Ashes, with their leaves yellow and brown

111

in the approach to the long, cold winter, I see the answer and wonder that I had not found it before.

Of course! Like Leah, I must write my message of love and send it to Maman. I shall obtain the name of the street where Jenny now lives and from which she writes to Papa. Did I not hear him growl the other day that "the wretched Colon" was after him again, for money (why I do not know, but it will concern the killing of Papa's rival, I am sure). So I may at last beg Maman to come to Thornfield and marry Papa, as she should have done long ago. My letter will be written today. There is a need for haste: I heard the conversation that took place in the garden last night, the confidences given by Papa, who now makes a habit of sharing all his thoughts with the governess I detest, little Miss Eyre.

Papa informed Miss Eyre that soon he will marry Mademoiselle Blanche. He wishes Jane to sit up with him all the night before his *mariage* — until the dawn comes into the sky — and this I cannot understand at all, for it was not in Papa's voice that he wishes to marry Mademoiselle Blanche.

I shall attempt to describe my own deceiving of Madame Fairfax, and perhaps some will think I have inherited my capacity for lies and cunning from the great Monsieur Rochester. For I am his daughter indeed, though he will on occasion deny it, for whichever reason comes into his head.

I waited until Leah had gone into the room Grace Poole calls the *boodwah* of Madame F — she carried towels or the like — and then I put my head around the door and smiled my very best smile at the old housekeeper. "Papa has asked me to provide a bouquet from my own hand for the chamber of Mademoiselle Ingram," said I (for the visit begins tomorrow: John and Mary, who make ready Ferndean Manor down in the damp woods for the servants of Mademoiselle Blanche and her mother, have said this is the "very last chance" of a betrothal between Papa and the haughty Miss Ingram, but I do not know what they mean). "I must gather the last roses from the walled garden while there is dew on them," I went on, clever as a monkey; and I could see that Madame F was convinced of the truth of what I said. "I will place them in the blue opaline vase Monsieur Rochester had as a *cadeau* from you," I finished off, and the custodian of Thornfield beamed, even if Leah winked at me, as she went out carrying in her arms a pile of newly laundered linen for the guests. "Don't be long," Madame F said, and I scampered away, blessed by the one person who had reason to tell me to mind my own business and get down to my bed. For Miss Eyre, as Madame F must know, is not indoors this evening: indeed, she is often called by the master (as John and Mary and Leah and Grace call him) to join him in the lime walk, or down by the ornamental pond. Sometimes he will take her to the rose garden, where I have said I will go tonight, to gather the last pink blooms with their frilly petals like the hem of the *robe* Papa brought me back from Paris, the beautiful dress chosen by Maman, as I know it must have been. Why Papa wishes to confide in Miss Eyre so frequently, I do not know. And last night, when it was growing dark and Jane was still not back in the schoolroom tidying the essays she makes me write and constructing the sums I cannot do, I decided to discover the reason for Papa's determination to tell his thoughts to the little governess.

"Then you are going to be married, sir?" These are the first words I heard, from Miss Eyre, for it had taken me some time to discover Papa and the young woman he employed to make a lady of the *fillette* sent over to him from Paris. I had found the pair in the laurel walk, at the very end by the sunken fence and the horse chestnut. I crept into a clump of bamboo — where Papa says a panther lives, and he gives a great breathing sound as I walk past with him, so I cry out in fear. But last night I found the courage to go into the bamboo myself, to hear what Papa has to say to the mousy governess.

"With your usual acuteness you have come straight to the point," says Monsieur Rochester to Jane — and I feel myself cold in there, in the tropical plant that would like to suffocate me with its long spears of prickly grass. Papa will marry? And soon? I hold my breath, as the panther likes to do before sighing out when we go by. "Very soon, my — that is, Miss Eyre: and you'll remember, Jane, the first time I, or rumor, plainly intimated to you that it was my intention to put my old bachelor's neck into the sacred noose, to enter into the holy state of matrimony — to take Miss Ingram to my bosom, in short (she's an extensive armful: but that's not the point — one can't have too much of such a very excellent thing as my beautiful Blanche). . . ."

I believe that Jane looked away for some reason at this point, and Monsieur Rochester, desiring to recapture her attention, leaned after her so that his words were lost to me. I heard only "you and little Adèle had better trot forthwith," followed later by "Adèle must go to school, and you, Miss Eyre, must get a new situation."

"Yes, sir, I will advertise immediately," came the governess's reply.

There was emotion in the air — there could scarcely not have been, with Papa announcing his intentions — but it was of myself, it goes without saying, that I thought with anguish and despair. I climbed from the back of the bamboo and held my nose to prevent my sneezes at the dust that flew in my face. My back and legs were scratched, and I began to hear myself sob as I ran over soft earth and then into the far end of the laurel walk, near the house I thought I would never love when first I came to Thornfield and which I now never want to leave. How can Papa send me away to school, when Maman will come here after my letter arrives in Italy, sent on to her by Jenny in Paris? How can he lose me as if I am no more to him than the little papillon spaniel, the lapdog Mademoiselle Blanche brings with her everywhere, even to Mr. Rochester's demesne, for she loves the dog a deal more than she loves Papa, that is for sure. How can he banish me, who sent for me to live with him at Thornfield?

Of Miss Eyre I did not think at all.

It is early in the morning, and I have not slept all night. I feel pride at my presence of mind, that on the way back to the house I dried my eyes and looked up at the great black windows of the Hall, assuring myself that it is my destiny to remain here, that one day Papa will love me all the time, and not just, as now, when his fancy takes him or he wishes to please Miss Eyre. Papa will be mine — and he will be Maman's also, when he tires of playing with a child and needs the mystery of a woman's love.

I went to the rose garden and picked the roses, as I had told Madame Fairfax I was going to do. There was no dew on them: the day had been dry and the evening dryer still, and as I took the thorns from my fingers, I did not shed tears. There was an eager, frightening feeling in the air, such as comes with the storms my poor friend Antoinette used to love watching, from her aerie high on the roof. The sky had grown very dark, and the last part of my return to the side door of the Hall I ran, in case the panther who lives in the bamboo down by the sunken fence had followed me all the way up to the rose garden.

I was afraid all night in my small *lit carré* and very awake. I knew I must act to stop this *mariage* between Papa and the "armful" he describes as Mademoiselle Blanche. Yet I have heard his voice, his manner of speaking, down by the horse chestnut tree, to Miss Eyre. He would speak in this way to Maman, before they would go to her *chambre à coucher* together — and sometimes he would pick her up in his arms and carry her in there. Then the door closed and the key turned in the lock. Why does Monsieur Rochester speak to the governess in this way? Does Papa not love Mademoiselle Blanche after all?

Whatever the answer may be — and Papa loves to tease; perhaps he imagines Jane hopelessly *amoureuse* of her employer and he makes fun of her, which I know is not kind — wherever the answer may lie, Papa has said he will marry as soon as possible; and as soon as possible Maman shall come here and put an end to this nonsense.

It is early, and the storm has raged all

night, so I run out into the garden and feel the wet grass under my feet. I go down the laurel walk, as if I can find Monsieur Rochester and the lovesick governess still there, she weeping from a broken heart and he extolling the perfections of his future bride.

But of course they are not there. I look around me, at the destruction brought by the storm. And I run indoors once more, up to the bright room with its chintz curtains and coverings, where I am more glad than I thought I would be to find Jane asleep in her narrow bed. "The chestnut tree at the bottom of the orchard has been struck by lightning in the night," I tell Jane, clambering into bed beside her and pulling at her brown hair. "Half of the tree is split away, mademoiselle. Come and see!"

The roses in the *grande chambre* that was made ready for the bride of Papa stand brown in the pretty vase, the curtains are drawn, and the fire in the grate stays unlit. For Mademoiselle Blanche will not come now, nor her mother who looks down her nose at the little French bastard of Monsieur Rochester, nor the young men and the girls with their dowries and their big skirts and their way of ogling Papa once Blanche is out of the room.

At the very last minute the visit was canceled. Cook is standing at the great range, and a haunch of venison comes out, to be basted, while John fetches port from the cellar for the mixture Maman would refuse if she was here and push away with an exclamation of disgust, the sauce they call Cumberland. Leah staggers under the weight of the potatoes that must roast in the oven, now that they are boiled, and as they are floury and gray when she heaves them to the long trestle table, I think longingly of Maman once again: for she would not have permitted *pommes de terre* of this nature in the house. Jenny would make a gratin, to accompany the leg of mutton Maman liked to serve when there was company on a Sunday, in the rue Vaugirard. To the thinly sliced potatoes Jenny would add cream, and a little cheese, the Gruyère from Switzerland, and a pinch of nutmeg. (But then, when I think of the nutmeg, I am reminded of my friend now imprisoned forever — so I must imagine — behind the cruel door Grace guards day and night on the third story of Thornfield Hall.) I have lost my mother and my *nouvelle amie* both; and to keep myself from

120

weeping before the whole kitchen staff, I have to lift an onion from the table and pretend to cut it for the other sauce Maman would never approve, the onion sauce as thick and white and filled with flour as everything else they eat in this strange Yorkshire. Even so, the onion is seized from me by Cook, and I am left to wipe my eyes on Leah's apron. The fact is, as I have to tell myself when further reprimanded by Mary and told to leave the kitchen and go find Mademoiselle Eyre to continue with my lessons, I am in my heart happy that the Ingram party has not come. Surely Papa will not wed a guest who refuses to attend the welcome party arranged in her honor? And — even if the rumor is true, that it is Papa who has called off the whole affair — then I cannot grieve long for his lack of *politesse*. He has seen he must not marry Mademoiselle Blanche: I am delighted that he has, even at the very last minute, come to his senses in this respect.

I skip to the far side of the immense kitchen at Thornfield and occupy myself with Bella the scullery maid there, as she shreds a mound of spinach still muddy from the garden. For Madame Fairfax has thrown open the window that separates the basement passage at Thornfield from the steamy room, lit by a great skylight, where Cook and her minions prepare the meals. She leans in, as she does daily, to give or countermand orders, the ribbons on her freshly starched bonnet tied tightly under her chin, so that her face resembles a scone, or another of the buns and floury marvels pulled out of the oven on a baking tray before the hour for tea. I am not in favor with Madame Fairfax, as I know well. She is pale and stares at me and Miss Eyre as we leave the schoolroom and depart on another journey with Monsieur Rochester, to Whitcross or Millcote, in search, it seems, of another reason for Monsieur Rochester to spend money on silks and satins for Miss Eyre, and for him also to tease me with his tales of going to the moon — for that is where he will go to live with Jane, so he says, and when I repeat this to Madame F, she shakes her head and looks grave indeed.

I know that Madame F understands that all Papa's gestures are for me. He pleases the governess in order to bring me happiness: he promises me dresses that will far outshine hers, because, *naturellement*, the dresses will come from Paris. If I miss lessons because Papa speaks with Jane, he speaks with her for that purpose: that I may enjoy my life here at Thornfield Hall. Madame Fairfax is *jalouse*, I daresay, of the preference for me over all others that her employer has recently shown. And if Miss Eyre looks at him like a moonstruck heifer in the barn where Jack takes me from time to time to milk the cows and pat their shiny black noses — then it is *tant pis* for her. She, too, will perforce understand the nature of Papa's love for his family, when Maman comes and our little circle is complete.

As if to prove that all the luck is with me now, Madame F singles me out for a smile as she looks in through the hatch window into the kitchen. Bella has to nudge me — Bella who mutters as she plunges the tough, mud-encrusted spinach into water that runs in cold from a great pipe leading to the water pond on the moor. Everyone knows that Bella is lacking something in her head; and she is no taller than I am, as we stand together by the big stone sink. She has one eye that is always closed, poor Bella, and she has to skew right around to try to tell me that the housekeeper, who controls all our lives here at Thornfield, wishes to speak to me straightaway.

Everyone stares as I go to the inner

window, and Madame F says I must follow her upstairs, no dawdling about it. But as she speaks the stern words, I see she favors me, just as Papa does these days. And because of their affection for me, Adèle is popular in Thornfield Hall. "Come now," Madame F says; and when we are up in the boudoir, she gives me a mug of the sweet pink drink she says is made from the rose hips that come plump and red on the rosebushes in the garden, when the flowers have died. As I sip, she sits me on a low velvet pouffe, of a grassy green that I think goes very well with the pantalettes I like to wear. She hands me a letter. My heart gives a violent leap when I see that it is from Jenny Colon — she who has not written for so many months, she who knows the whereabouts of Maman. "Your Parisian friend has written to me, as you see," says Madame Fairfax, and her voice is gentle. "She informs me that Madame Varens will come here this month. You will be pleased to see your mother, little Adèle, I have no doubt."

This time I cannot keep the hot tears from streaming down my face. I do not listen to Madame Fairfax as she goes on. Maman comes here; the bad part of the fairy tale has come to an end; we shall live happily ever after, Maman, Papa, and I.

"So you will be able to continue your life in Paris when your Maman has taken you back there," says Madame F — but I do not hear her at all when she says this over and over, for the room is filled with the bright light of my happiness, and I no longer care if the plain Yorkshire sky outside the window has as many animal-shaped clouds as a Noah's ark in an infant's dream. And, for all the strictness she has shown me in the past, I now feel only love for Madame Fairfax, and I promise myself I will be *une sage petite fille* and do whatever the good housekeeper asks of me.

For what Madame Fairfax does not yet know is that Maman comes to this great château to marry Papa. He knows she comes, and he has canceled the betrothal party with Mademoiselle Ingram for that reason. They will marry in the chapel, and I shall wear the organdy that is the color of the peaches in Papa's greenhouse up beyond the kitchen garden.

We shall all live together at Thornfield. And Miss Eyre may stay to continue my education — if Maman approves it, that is to say.

Seven

Grace

Here's the story of how a good plan can misfire — a plan, that is, that would have made Grace Poole rich and would have rid the master of his problem, if nature had been allowed to take its course.

This is what took place: I went down to the master's room this morning and told him his wife was gone again — gone and not coming back this time by the looks of it — and good riddance to her as far as you're concerned, I wanted to say, though it didn't pay me to do so.

It was early, for gentry at any rate, with Leah still cooking the breakfast for Mrs. F. "Oh, I'll just take a little porridge, and no cream whatever you do," the silly old woman says, and then I catch her guzzling the preserved plums in the master's silver box on the sideboard. "Oh, Leah, the cambric pillowcases weren't properly ironed yesterday — surely that nincompoop of a maid can learn how to use a steam iron? I don't want Miss Ingram with damp or creased dresses." And so on and on, while I'm waiting right up in the eaves for the plain stuff Mrs. R gets given, and me along with her. "No, you cannot cook for yourself up there," Mr. R says when I ask for a small pantry — surely it wouldn't be too much, and then I could boil or roast in the room the master calls "Grace's room," though God knows it's not mine to dispose of or even leave. "We don't want fire up there," Mr. R says. And he looks away in that end-of-the-world way he has, as if being master of all isn't enough to keep him cheerful most of the time.

So today I had to wait, till Leah had come up with the gruel and set it down, bad-tempered in all her ways as ever, on the table in "Grace's room," the room with windows so high up in the eaves you can't look out at Thornfield land or see whether it's snow or rain today.

"What is it, Grace?" my mistress — if that's what you'd call her, the wretched Creole the master brought back here from the sugar estates his father had ("It's all tobacco now, Cousin Fairfax," I heard him say some years back, but if you ask me, they're still slaves just like we are here at Thornfield Hall) — the poor white woman calls out to me as she always does. "What is it, Grace? Are they my fruits, pineapple and mango and lime? Is there a hibiscus blossom on the tray? Am I home at last?"

You can't help feeling sorry for this wife the master has made a prisoner of, but on a cold, dark morning it just grates on my nerves to have the woman he calls his "Antoinette" crying for all those exotic things she'll never taste again. And now she's locked up in her cell every hour of the night and day, after the fright we had with her lately. Yet it's true, her escaping like that did give me the idea of making my fortune at last, from the crazy creature I've watched over so long. "No, Bertha," says I, "it's the gruel. And there's an apple here. From the orchard where you used to like to go walking when you first came to Thornfield — remember?"

Then she falls silent, and this is very probably the last exchange we'll have — unless Mrs. F comes up and I tell the madwoman to stop her babbling. If it gets so bad the master has to be called for, he'll "recommend a cold bath." Oh, that makes Mrs. R holler, all right, and cruel it is, too, with the prisoner bundled down to the yard where they hose the horses and given a fair beating with a spray of icy water at full throttle. I've seen Mr. R leave the house when this punishment is going on, and I don't blame him. I'd leave myself, if I could. "It's not because of you I stay here," I say to the poor lunatic when she clings to me and cries for a hug or some other proof of affection. "There's nowhere for me to go," and I ram the point home. And then I know she knows I see Thornfield Hall as just as much of a prison as she does. We belong to a master who'd happily see us dead — that I tell her sometimes, too. And then she cries as if her heart would burst open.

Today it was all going to be different. Mr. R's "fiancée," as they call her in the servants' hall (where John and Mary are too stuck up to let me eat with them), was expected today. Her second visit in just a matter of weeks. She was due to be the new mistress of the Hall, the queen of his heart, so they say.

And the only one who knows an impediment to the marriage of Miss Blanche Ingram and Mr. Edward Fairfax Rochester ("impediment" is a fine word, and it was Bertha's brother, Mr. Mason, who first taught it to me) is Grace Poole.

We were in the room with the high windows, Mr. Richard Mason and I, on the occasion of his last visit to Thornfield. I know he comes here to get money from the master, and I soon set myself to learn his tricks. "You and I, we're the only ones who know the secret," the gentleman from the West Indies says to me, after pouring me a glass of Tokay he's brought up from the cellars, cool as cucumber. "You'll like this better than that evil porter you tope, Grace," says Mr. Mason, and he gives a high-pitched laugh that almost wakes Bertha — though I'd given her enough laudanum to keep her still at least a day or two. "Mrs. F would never tell the world the shame of my sister's confined state," Bertha's brother goes on, "and the decline of her mental powers; dear Mrs. Fairfax would not care to be kin to a man like Edward, who could reduce his lawfully wedded wife to little more than an animal."

As Mr. Mason said the words "lawfully wedded wife," I saw his meaning. If the master so much as began to believe he could remarry, then the blackmail would begin in earnest. Mr. Mason would end up a rich man. Why he imagines I wouldn't go in for this game, too, I cannot say. I didn't count, I suppose: I was just Grace Poole.

Well, the week of the confirmation of

Miss Blanche Ingram as official fiancée to Mr. Edward Fairfax Rochester came, and it saw a great upheaval and bustling at Thornfield. This time, as we all knew at the Hall, the master had to declare his intentions; he'd put those diamonds back in the safe too often, as Cook and Leah agree. Mary, Mr. R's devoted servant, was at sixes and sevens over the bed linen and the hip baths, and with John shouting at the lads down in the lower regions to stoke the boiler up high and Mrs. F speaking coldly to that sharp-eyed little minx Leah, it was a busy scene at Thornfield and no mistaking.

But Mr. Richard Mason, as I noticed and I was all the happier for it, had missed the cue entirely. No sign of a telegram, no figure just off the coach at Whitcross walking up the drive with gold written all over his face. No voice at the bottom of the stairs to the attic, soft and cooing like the wood pigeons that fly about the woods on the far hill of the Ingram estates. "Grace, are you there?" I'd think I heard it sometimes — but as the days passed, I began to see that the road was open to me alone. And I began to form my plan.

Bertha was in one of her heavy sleeps

when I took her from the trundle bed. She sometimes wakes and thinks she's in her marital couch, on honeymoon in those accursed spice islands she paid the master to take her away from. Then, when she sees the narrow iron bedstead and the high, sloping walls without so much as a chink of light, she groans and rolls over. On this occasion I made sure she rolled right into the net — or hammock, if you like: I came across it in the attic where the playthings of Master Edward and his late, lamented brother were stored once they grew too old to have a use for them.

She looked like something from that exotic place I thought I'd never see — Bequia, sounded like its name. "Grace, you'd love the Windward Islands" — so poor Bertha would croon sometimes, and tell me of the nutmegs and breadfruit a Captain Cook had planted there, on an island I like the sound of, along with plants with fronds and spiky leaves such as Mr. R's new bride would give her eyes for, in the new greenhouses down by the water garden at Thornfield. "Let me tell you about the trade winds, Grace."

Today, lying in that bright hammock on the floor of the attic room she's been in more years than anyone could care to count, the wife of Mr. Rochester looked like something that's turned from a butterfly back to a caterpillar, and I couldn't help wishing I didn't have to do this to her — though she knew nothing, thanks to Quincey's drops, of her destination or her future life. I muttered a few words to her, as if it would give her some comfort, as I dragged her down the stone spiral stairs (I knew that Mrs. F had gone all the way to Sheffield, visiting her niece, and this I considered was the best part of my good luck today).

While I was muttering on — and thinking who was the madwoman here now, I heard Leah's footsteps running heavy as always up the small staircase you can reach only by going behind the tapestry — the ghost's stairs, we call it — to the third story of the house. She'd already cleared the gruel tray. I hadn't bargained for this. And I wished I hadn't enjoyed the gin the way I had last night, for I was sweating like a pig by the time I'd pushed poor Bertha into the log cupboard outside the room Mrs. F calls her *boodwah*. It was a long way down, from the log store through the skylight into the tower room below — but I'd opened the creaking joists of the skylight the day before and placed a pile of old rugs on the floor, for poor Bertha to drop on.

After all, we want her alive and not dead. And from the tower room I could drag her onto the cart and climb on behind, like when John goes into Whitcross on an errand. I was muffled up and hooded. It's a risk, but it's one I was ready to take. On a day like this, with the arrival of a new bride for the master, Bertha was worth her weight in the proverbial lucre.

"You're out of breath, Leah," I said to the lass when she came pounding down the hidden staircase onto the landing — and, to my horror, made for the log cupboard. No doubt Mary had told her Miss Blanche Ingram will be wanting a roaring fire in her room as soon as she comes in. A fire is permitted for the future mistress of Thornfield so long as she's bringing a good dowry and a few thousand acres of land, I said to myself — though what I was really thinking is what to do about Leah if she tried to enter that log cupboard outside Mrs. F's room. "I *observed* you last night, my girl," I said, banking on the fact that Leah is a slut of the first order and I'd already seen her with the new stable lad a couple of times. It's well known that Mrs. Fairfax will not tolerate what she calls "improper behavior" at Thornfield; and when she *observes* it — a word I knew would come in useful for me one day — then it's out on your ear whether the snow's coming down or not.

Leah turned and looked at me, then fled back down the stairs. I was free — free to take my prisoner to the hideaway I had set up for her, free to end my own life sentence in this cursed house, and free to make my proposition to the master and grow rich. I've lived long enough without a ray of light coming into my life, that's true enough, and there's plenty here can bear witness to it, from Leah to Mary and John, and even Mrs. F herself I've caught looking at me pityingly.

But today I knew for the first time my luck would change — and for the first time since I could remember, I'd say there wasn't a cloud in the sky.

The master didn't need any explaining to when I knocked on the door of his room bright and early. (We'd been "up" for hours, my poor crazy charge and me, but what does that count for when there's nowhere to go but around the room and back to bed again? At least today I'd had work to do, lugging the wretch down the stairs.) But — when you come to think of it —

wouldn't it be enough to drive anyone mad, the way he shut her up there when she began to complain of cold and all manner of illnesses: "Get up, Antoinette," Mr. R used to say in the old days when he still had some hope for the woman from Port of Spain. "Get up, or I'll make sure this is the last time you'll have the pleasure of my company!"

It was something like that he'd say, and it just made matters worse for the shivering woman in the dark room where he put her almost as soon as they came back from Jamaica and the honeymoon to those islands she liked to talk about, the islands with the nutmegs and the passionflowers she wore in her hair. "Get up, Antoinette. . . ."

Now it was *his* turn to get up quickly and follow me up the stairs. He knew there mustn't be a repeat of trouble on the day Miss Blanche comes, and her mother along with her, who never once looks you in the eye if you're a servant or a keeper — which is just what the master don't want them to know I am.

He followed me without saying a word. I know the man well enough to tell when his schemes going wrong will send him into one of his rages, and I reckoned he was holding on as hard as he could, not to explode with temper as we went up to the third story. It *would* be today — I did hear him mumble those words. He wants Miss Blanche's land, of course — and anything that gets in the way of money for Mr. R has to be stamped on pretty quickly. All the same, he knows I hold the secret — and the other one who would be interested to know that Mr. R was plotting bigamy was right across the world, a big, cold ocean away.

We walked into "Grace's Room" together, and I had to hold my sides to stop from laughing when I saw him screw up his eyes to get used to the poor light up there before going through to the cell where Antoinette has lived close on fifteen years. Was he going to start up again? It's as if the man can't be with a woman without going back to the days when they were lovers. "Antoinette, my darling, how are you today?" he said, just as I'd imagined he would. But he didn't stay that way for long — it's only when her brother Mr. Mason is here that he holds back, and today, as I knew he would, he started upbraiding his own evil fortune, before storming out of the attic rooms in a rage.

Today, as it happens, Bertha Mason — or Mrs. Rochester, whom no one is permitted to know exists — is a mile or so away in a hayloft prepared by myself to receive her. A bribe to the new stable lad did it — his father is the cowman on the outlying farm at Millcote — and lips will be sealed if anyone stumbles across a woman closed up in there with the hay. Mr. R is a tight-fisted employer, and the family is glad of the money I handed over, from my savings. "There'll be more of it if you keep your mouth shut, Jack," I said. By my reckoning, what I've handed over will keep them quiet no more than two weeks. But by then Mr. R would be paying — and he'd be doubling my money thereafter till I was ready to go. (I had a mind to go south, to where my sister lives, near the sea in Devon. She'd be glad enough to see me if I brought the gold I'm claiming — but all this belongs in the land of make-believe by now.)

"Grace, where is your mistress?" said Mr. R. I had to stop myself from laughing at the way his voice trembled.

"I don't know, sir," I said. And honestly, as I turned to face him, I believed myself. It couldn't be true that the bride he had brought to the Hall with such lovely dresses, with combs and diamonds piled in her hair, could be locked in a foul-smelling barn along with rotting bales of hay and a couple of cows Jack had brought in there last night, breaking his word that my prisoner would be alone. Not that I'm surprised at what he did. If he was getting paid for the hay — as I'd told him he would be — why not make good use of it for the cow and her calf? We're all the same under the skin, and there's not so much difference between the stable lad and the master of Thornfield Hall when you come down to it.

Just looking at Mr. R's face as it dawned on him that his wife was out there again, roaming and a danger to the prospects of his new marriage, was worth a sovereign or two. But I waited — and here is where I showed myself as a chump who deserves all the bad luck that's coming, and more — before bringing up the reward I had in mind. Later, I figured, when Miss Blanche and her mother were shown to their rooms and Mr. R was hopping with nerves that poor Bertha would come walking in at any moment of the night or day — that was when I'd make my offer to Mr. R to stay quiet on the subject of the first Mrs. Rochester. More fool me.

Well, there wasn't much time to spare for this "eligible bachelor" — those being the words I'd heard Mrs. F use about her cousin and employer, as if she had to go on pretending she'd never guessed what really lay beyond "Grace's Room" upstairs. The master of Thornfield had to get himself ready for the visitors and appear in charge of the ceremonies when he greeted them on this all-important visit.

"Very well, Grace," came the snapped reply to my protest that I'd no idea where his dearly beloved could be. "You were hired to guard over Miss Antoinette" — he can't bring himself to say "my wife"; I don't praise him for his cowardice in that — "to guard her and care for her," Mr. R went on, and I heard the beginnings of the storm of his famous temper building far off on the shores of what he calls his "patience and forbearing." Soon the cyclone would hit — and even Mrs. F would run from her room, scurrying down to the Hall to avoid a good lashing from her master's tongue. "How *dare* you?" shouted Master Edward, as he was called before the sad death of his elder brother, good Master Rowland. "How were you so careless? Drunk, I suppose?"

The pitch of his voice was awful. But then it dropped again. We stood there, in the room with the high windows where he's made me lose my own youth, unable to look out at the world unless I stand on the chair by the attic window, incapable of love or entertainment, and with only gin or a porter mug for company.

We looked each other in the eye. Whether he knew I knew the whereabouts of his wife, I cannot say. But he was quiet as a mouse all of a sudden, and then he turned on his heel and left the room. If anyone was all churned up, you could say it was I, Grace Poole. I'd expected him to rant and rave. But he went down the stairs like a gentleman. The visit of Miss Blanche wouldn't be spoiled for him, not yet.

And an hour or so later, when I'd worked at carrying the ewers and jugs of water to the rooms and piled coals on the fires in the library and the Hall as if nothing had happened (and indeed, as the existence of my charge was a secret, nothing had), I was there at the back by the servants' staircase to watch the gentry arriving. I had to hear from Miss Eyre, the governess, that the visit of Blanche Ingram and her mother had been canceled — surely for the last time, I thought when I saw Mr. Rochester's face, black as thunder. She was in his confidence, certainly. Now if he'd just given me the chance to speak to him —

141

very well, to blackmail him, if you like — things would have gone swimmingly for both of us.

When things didn't go as I planned, I put it down to the bad luck the little French girl had brought to Thornfield, with her talk of an old witch fortune-teller she visits in the "pretty, clean town" she left, to come and be with her Papa.

Mind, she didn't call him that at first. The poor child didn't know what to expect at Thornfield Hall; and I will own that the lies I told to that affected little piece of Paris frippery made everything worse in the end. But she made me think she could look into the future — that the old woman in Paris she told me about with the toad and the black cat really had picked her as some kind of special seer into the future. And I badly wanted to know when the best moment would be, for going to the master and saying I'd reveal the existence and whereabouts of his wife if he didn't pay up. For, even with the engagement to Miss Ingram no longer a possibility, I reckoned it would still be worth something to Mr. Rochester to get rid of the anxiety over his mad wife's movements. Although of course I didn't put it like that to little Miss Adela

— I made it sound like a romantic tie and the need to approach a man of the world for advice when all had gone sour on us.

"Oh, I do not know, Grace," Adela said. She pronounced my name like "ass," and it made me laugh. I could see that Mrs. F was irritated by the child, the "ward" of Mr. R — and she wouldn't take my remarks on the subject, either. Mrs. F had to be proper at all times. But, for all the housekeeper's dislike of the foolish creature, I came to enjoy the company of Adela. I had the feeling I could use her one way or another, if not in the spirit world then simply as one who was close to the master. The fact that he seemed bored with his "little bastard," as I heard him describe her to the governess out in the garden under the big tree, didn't put me off for long. Blood will out, with the gentry — even if this sprig looked as unlike her father as it was possible to be.

"I believe you must find a good time in your heart," said the child, who likes to spout such nonsense when she comes to my room high in the house and sits on the poorly made wooden chair that is the sole furniture apart from my table and my own hard perch. "La Cibot tells me you must find the tarot card that is your sign, and you must learn from that." Adela shrugs. Again it amuses me to see a child as much like a miniature woman as this one. But I don't have these cards she talks of — and I soon dozed off when she ran on about the arcades she loves in Paris, and the man called Félix who takes her to his studio and lets her watch him making men's faces on paper, growing them, she says, in a great tank with a strange-smelling liquid inside. I wonder at the life she's led already, with her mother dancing, she says, over the heads of the crowd in the circus ring. A *danseuse de corde* — Adela makes me repeat the name of her mother's profession — trapeze acrobat, I daresay, though when the fair came to Millcote, I was the one left behind here at Thornfield. They said the master didn't want me to go. Only I knew the reason: poor mad Bertha might have escaped while I gasped at the high-wire dancers and laughed at the clowns.

I like to picture little Adela's mother as she swings high above the crowd. The child takes my mind off my worries, but I can't get away from thinking that everything is not turning out as it should. The worst feeling I have, which of course Adela can never guess, is that the master knows exactly what I have done and the blackmail

I still intend to practice on him, whether he makes it up with Miss Blanche or not. I should have demanded ransom money earlier, when the visit of Miss Blanche was just about to happen. And now that the master has lost his nerve and canceled it, what am I to do with my prisoner who is in the barn, beyond the stable buildings? How can I speak to Mr. Rochester? For he never mounts to the third story now, or sees me when I walk past. Grace Poole has become the ghost of Thornfield Hall.

The worst of it is that Antoinette is weak and, I fear, dying in the hayloft. I had to move her to the uppermost bales when Jack walked in and brought another cow with him, pointing out that the money for renting the broken-down old barn was running out. And there is worse still: the child Adela has heard — from Leah doubtless, but she will have been told not to say — that there is a "strange woman" living somewhere in a barn just beyond the park fence. And that I, Grace Poole, will show her to the curious child. So the net tightens, and the fear begins to mount inside me. Grace Poole will end up dangling from a rope if the luck don't change soon — that I know.

Eight

Adèle

There was a house in Paris at the time of the *douceur de vivre* Maman would tell me about — a time she said she despised, before we in France were set free — where the rich old aristocrat owner kept a byre (as Jack the stable lad calls it) right in the elegant first story of his mansion. "There was hay, and a couple of cows munching peacefully, and the old man had his rustic dream fulfilled," Maman said; and she laughed at the *folies* and extravagances of the nobility in our country in those days before Madame Guillotine was invented for the purpose of cutting off their heads. "The marquis," Maman continued with a faraway look in her eyes (so I thought for a moment that Céline had in fact been contented with the ancien régime, as it is known to the republicans liberated by Monsieur Robespierre and his kind) "the marquis had a boy to milk the animals, and he lay reading in bed in the midst of this farmyard scene. Can you imagine it?"

Maman and Jenny used to laugh at this point, as they remembered the eccentricities of the old days. And it is their laughter I think of now, after climbing into the hayloft where I paid Leah to take me, with the louis d'or Jenny sent me for a time when I might need to run away from Thornfield or otherwise save my life. In my opinion it is as important as my own life to rescue my friend Antoinette — for when Leah giggled and told me there was a strange woman found high on the bales in the barn at the far end of the park, I knew this stranger was the *bonne amie* I had on the roof at Thornfield, the kind woman with long black hair who sang me songs of her far-off island.

Leah knew about my little store of gold (for Nadar had given me a sovereign, payment for a photograph of a rich *anglais,* he said), and I knew that Leah wanted the money in order to help her to marry Jack, for she is *enceinte* with his child, so she says.

I had formed my plan to slip out of the house yesterday — the day when the good thing happened: Papa's planned marriage to Mademoiselle Blanche was called off; and then the bad thing came after, when Miss Eyre called me into the schoolroom and told me she had news for me that will affect all of our lives very much.

At first Jane paced the schoolroom in silence, and, as a fine evening lay outside, I had promised Leah to meet her — with the louis d'or in my pinafore pocket, *naturellement* — at the gate to the park from the garden; from there we would have only a short walk to the hayloft, where I thought of my friend, like the Parisian aristocrat, reclining on pillows and sipping creamy milk. Why Jane walked back and forth with so agitated an air, I did not like to wonder. But later, as I reflect, this was the first time the eyes of the little governess shone so bright that one was made to think of their color as green and not the dull "hazel" she has told me they are, when I have asked her what the word is in English for such an uninteresting *regard*. "Adèle," said Jane, coming over to me at last and taking me in her arms (and this I have learned not to refuse, for there is a scent of fresh lime I shall forever associate with my little governess: it is as if she is half tree, half woman, like the drawings of the mythological creatures I find sometimes in the big books in Papa's library), "my dear Adèle," Jane said as she stooped low over me and I breathed in the green

148

leaves that waft from her. "I shall be married tomorrow. We would invite you to attend the ceremony, but it is for us alone — and then we will be away a time, leaving Thornfield immediately afterward. You will be a good girl — you will do all Mrs. Fairfax says. Promise me now, my dear!"

I promised, as my mentor was extremely eager for me to do so; and then, as I was suddenly overcome by shyness, I found I could not ask the name of the bridegroom. I stood as tongue-tied as Little Jack Horner in his corner — while the minutes ticked away, and Leah must have scuffed her feet with impatience on the stableyard cobbles, waiting for me to appear. "I marry Mr. Rochester," Jane said quietly as I remained rooted to the spot for what seemed an age. "I could not tell you before, Adèle, as he did not wish it. But I may assure you that I intend to be very happy indeed!" And with that, the girl who was no longer the mousy Miss Eyre bounded across the schoolroom to the window and looked out at the forecourt of Thornfield Hall, as if certain her betrothed would now come riding up there.

As for me, I fled from the room and down the back stairs to the door that leads out to the stable buildings, as fast as I could go. Cross, and in the act of stomping off, Leah needed a sight of the louis d'or — which she fished for in the pocket of my overalls as if I were no more than a common thief handing over stolen booty in return for a reward. She pulled my hair, too, did Leah, so I snuffled and sobbed all the way across the shortcut in the park, the overgrown path that leads to the barn where Jack keeps his two cows.

Nine

Grace

So there is to be a wedding at Thornfield Hall after all! Leah came to tell me at dawn; and I own I went straight down to the cellar and took hold of a bottle of the master's port, for Grace is in worse trouble now, and no mistaking it.

But there were other matters here to be solved: how did my mistress — another way of describing the poor woman kept at my pleasure in the hayloft until I take my courage in my hands and make the owner of the Hall pay up — guess the existence of this new light in the eye of the master? How did she know that the man she married and set up for life, with her money from Jamaica, now had designs on a penniless orphan? The answer is simple: she saw them together in the garden from her lookout on the roof of the Hall — and my own wits are deserting me if I didn't see it earlier. But now, what with my concerns over the health of the wretched Creole and my fear she'd be discovered in the barn, I never thought to look under my own nose for the latest object of the master's affections. He can't be without a woman, and the chance his wife might turn up out of the blue one day has scared him off proposing to Miss Blanche. I was right there, and I should have understood he'd stick as near as possible to home when looking for the next one. But Miss Eyre! Eighteen years old! My only wonder is what the little governess will think when Adela, who has never kept her secrets for more than a day, explains to her dear Jane that love for the master, who is already a married man, is strictly forbidden by the church. Once Adela learns the secret, that is.

Of course, the lawfully wedded wife of Mr. Rochester simply saw it all for herself. Just as I thought the poor, drugged woman had been too weak to stir from her bed to the window; I found she'd been looking down and spying on them — something in the new song the master sings to the governess must have given strength to a failing woman. But Antoinette has always had powers that are disconcerting, and I have proof now that the cunning of the woman is just as the master describes. I would say she can make herself invisible, with those black arts she practiced in the islands across the sea — and on occasion she's been as impossible to pin down as the light that flickers out on the moor sometimes, when it's a hot summer night. One minute she's like a dead woman walking — the next minute she's gone. She'll climb out onto the roof and try to pull you down with her, I said to myself. But it turned out I needn't have worried that Miss Adela would go running to the lord and master with stories of the madwoman on the roof. She's easily distracted, and I can't say she knows the difference between what's there and what's not.

The little Parreesienne clambers on my knee and begins to tell me again about her beautiful Maman, the woman who left her own daughter just like that with only the street to look forward to as a home and went off to Italy. Sometimes we get even more of the famous Céline Varens: "Maman and Papa were in the white villa by the sea!" says Adèle, as she wants us to call her, French as you like with her long brown curls and her pale face. You can see she's bred of a woman who never did a real day's work in her life. "Villa, what villa?" I say, for I own I don't know the word. We don't have villas in this part of the world.

"In the sun," Adela says, and she sighs. "Papa and Maman are in the *grande chambre à coucher* —"

"Oh," say I, "I'll tell you one thing, my child. It's better to watch out for the traps in life as they come for you day by day than to go on dwelling on the past."

"And Maman is saying to Papa why she will not marry him," the child goes on. "She will change her mind now, I am sure of it. I have asked Madame Fairfax to write to Maman, to tell her Papa loves her still and she must return here to be with her family."

Poor child! If I didn't have such a deal of anxieties on my mind, I'd feel sorry for her. Whatever is going to befall Adèle Varens when the master marries Jane Eyre? But it's refreshing to hear of a woman who wouldn't marry Mr. Rochester, rather than the other way around. "Why wouldn't she accept the offer?" says I, as Adela wanted me to do. The whole story was very likely invented anyway, as Adela makes up with her lying for all the lessons she misses with the governess. "Maman told Papa she does not believe he understands the new French thinking," replied Adela in her important way. It'll surprise no one to hear I didn't inquire what this new French thinking might be. But Adela went on without caring if I wanted the answer or not. *"Liberté, Egalité, Fraternité,"* says the little wretch, and leaps from my knee. *"Liberté, Egalité —"*

"That's enough, child," I said, and I swiped at her as she ran past like the gnat she is, a nuisance to all of us here at Thornfield Hall. All the same, the idea of the master being refused on account of not understanding liberty or equality — why, even poor Grace Poole can fathom the meaning of those words. And — though I didn't own it to the child, I took my hat off to her mother, Céline Varens. Mr. R can go after his governess, with her yes, sirs and no, sirs, but he can't get a true equal like the Frenchwoman to agree to live by his side.

All of this took up my thoughts, and I hardly listened as Adela prattled on — though suddenly I had the need to ask very forcefully that she repeat what she said, slowly and without all those words in French.

"Antoinette *doit mourir,"* Adela said slowly in a loud voice, disobedient as usual. "She must die, so Papa can be free."

"What do you mean?" I cried. "This ain't a game, you know. You shouldn't speak of anyone in that way, child. Who have you been talking to? Now you must tell the truth."

"But yes, *la vérité*," the child said, serious now that she heard my tone and saw the expression on my face. I put my hands over my ears in the rush of horror that came after hearing her like this. Then I thought to myself that if anyone did murder the wretched Bertha, it was likely to be this little minx, with all her false affection and airs.

"Leah has told me," Adela sobbed, trying to climb onto my knee. But I wouldn't have it, I was rigid, and I must have appeared a ghost to her myself, for she began to cry in earnest, calling on "Maman" to help her from this horrible place.

"Well, Adela," I said. "First, how do you know who this woman is? And where have you seen her? Then I will see what you fabricate and what is true." And I lifted my hand, to show I'd give her a great slap if she lied, which only sent her into screams and hysterics worse than before.

At the end of it all, my very worst fears were confirmed. Leah in her idiot way had gone to romp in the hay bales with the stable lad Jack, and she'd seen poor Bertha there, moaning no doubt and begging to be allowed back to Thornfield Hall. The stories had come out — the Lord knows I'm sick enough of them — the hibiscus and the nutmegs on the island with the black sand where she went after she married and was for a short time happy. Her long years in the attics of the Hall. Her escape from the hayloft a day or two back and how she had seen "her Edward" and the little governess in the garden together. And so it had been Leah and Jack, part from spite against the wardress who had looked after the crazy woman so long — myself, Grace Poole — and part out of pity for me, who had set up little Adela to bring her back into the Hall.

Leah told Adela; of course she would and did. You never can gauge the amount of love a child will have for its mother or father — or both in this case, as it appears Adela still thinks she can bring them together at last at Thornfield Hall. "Now Papa will understand the French thinking," said the child, when she saw I wouldn't take her in my arms and pet her, as I had been known to do before. "And he can marry Maman when he is — as you say — *veuf*," Adela went on. "A widower," I said, and saw all my future fall out the window if the Creole woman died while under my care — and a jail sentence, too, unless I ran fast from Thornfield and found work elsewhere. I confess my mind was going as fast as the merry-go-round at Whitcross Fair, trying to see a way out of the deadly dangerous corner I was now in.

"And Maman will come very soon," cried Adela just as I had decided to get as fast as my legs would carry me to the old teacher in Millcote who'll write letters for those who can't read or write — like your poor Grace Poole. A letter needed to go — and I see it fly across the ocean and come down like a racing pigeon on the island with nutmegs I always put Antoinette on, in my mind. Her brother, Richard Mason, needed to come here quick — to stop the wedding of the master and the little governess. Mason it was who held proof of that first ceremony in Jamaica: who would listen to Grace Poole? And it was known here that Mr. Rochester and his new bride were going on a long wedding journey once the service is over — with Antoinette as miserably weak as she was when I last saw her in the barn, she'd be dead by the time they returned, and Grace would swing for her pains. Yes, Mr. Mason must come before the lecher Mr. R had got himself to church with that self-satisfied little piece Jane Eyre. Do you know of an impediment? Yes, Grace knows the word. Richard knows of an impediment, most certainly he does. "And what shall I wear when Maman is *épousée* with Papa?" the child keeps saying again and again, until I think I'm going to take leave of my senses. "The new rose satin Papa brought me from Paris? Or the gauze which is *transparent*, like a fairy's wings, the wings I had when I was in the Funambules Theater . . . ?"

I suppose something snapped in me. I don't see myself as cruel, in the ordinary run of business at any rate. Yes, I'd punish Bertha when she grew too Antoinette for my tastes — cloying and full of contradictory demands, acting like the forgotten queen. But I've never spoken just to bring hurt — something I did then, and it's too late to feel regret. "Your Maman isn't coming here, to Thornfield Hall," I said. That bit was true at least, there was no question so far as I could see, of an actress who's happy with a new lover — and probably another of the same sex as well, for all I know, this Jenny the child keeps talking of — settling down here with Edward Fairfax Rochester. She wouldn't find the equality and liberty she talks of in this country — no, she would not. And it's clear she said good-bye to her daughter when she ran off to Italy. There are enough women moiling and toiling around this place, each with her own wants and needs — from the governess Jane Eyre to Blanche Ingram still keeping hope alive to Bertha Mason herself, who'll be back here soon, you can mark my words. The money I gave Jack is running out, and he'll do no favors for me, that's certain. *No* French trapeze dancers here, please! I turned to Adela, who was practicing dance steps under the high window in my room. "Your Maman won't be coming to Thornfield, my child," I said. "Your Papa is marrying Miss Eyre, and it's time you came to terms with it, my child."

"Papa will marry Maman," Adela said.

Ten

Adèle

It was all like a dream, from the hour I went into the hayloft with Leah and she turned the pocket of my gingham pinafore inside out, so the gold coin rolled onto the barn floor and came to rest where Jack was standing, Jack who does not smile at Leah anymore, but keeps raking the hay and forking it to the cows in their stall.

Antoinette was like someone in a dream also, when I clambered up to find her, low in the bales of hay. She looked at me as if she knew me and didn't know me, like dream people do; and, as she acted strangely, I was frightened and understood I also knew nothing of this woman Leah calls a *folle* — and that she might put her hands, which are a yellowish color and very large, with dark fingernails such as I have never seen, around my neck and throttle me to death. So I crept back a little in the sweet-smelling hay and pretended that I was in Paris in the old *douce* days before the Terror of which Jenny speaks with such triumph in her voice. I thought of Maman's story, and of the rich old man with his private dairy in the middle of the city, and I wished Antoinette would laugh and cry *"mon doudou"* as she used to do. But, as I say, she gazed at me most suspiciously and it was as if we had never been friends at all.

"Now, take the crazy woman back to the Hall with you," Jack shouts from a long distance down at the foot of the hay mountain in the barn. "And no squealing to the master, or you'll get a taste of this," he calls, brandishing his rake, while Leah tries to hush him — afraid, I suppose, that I will go to Madame F and tell her of all the goings-on at her employer's farm. "And be quick about it," Jack goes on yelling. He has the louis d'or in his breeches pocket now, and I know from all those fights at the *cirque d'hiver,* when Maman walked the wire, that money will make people feel as powerful as a king, even if they gamble or drink it all away that same night.

So I had to pull the madwoman down from the hay, and neither Leah nor Jack looked at us as we hobbled out into the yard, and then beyond into the darkening park. It was horrible, going under trees that were tall and strange, like the figure, so thin by now you could see the bones stick out under her soiled dress as she walks. Antoinette had become a witch, her arms as long as the branches that waved in the mounting wind. When a leaf from the great beech tree in the park fell on her head, the crazy woman did not attempt to brush it off. She went on, her eyes staring as if the grass and the palisade and the few deer grazing by the sunk fence, held a horror for her, one that nobody else could see. And — for the first time — I wished Jane were here, she who sees the world as it really is, and who plays chess and checkers with me until it is long after my bedtime.

Jane . . . as we opened the wicket gate I knew also for the first time that I should miss her when she was gone away with Papa, and that it was also true that she loved him and he loved her in return. They could not marry, though — they could not marry, and Maman was on her way to Thornfield, as Jenny wrote just a few days ago in the letter Madame Fairfax read aloud to me. It was right that I tell Jane — for she had begged me to stay with her all night tonight, the night before her *mariage* — that Maman would come and would not expect to find her *mari* with the young woman employed at Thornfield as a governess. I should inform Jane as kindly as I could; and she would put away the fine veil she took suddenly from a drawer in the schoolroom, before I ran out to meet Leah and make my visit to the barn.

As it happened, everything that took place after my return to the Hall was as strange as the woman I brought with me, she who was "my Antoinette" and who became, once she reached the Hall — as if the magic they practice on her island had taken away her real self — simply Bertha, a zombie who walked quietly to her cell and sat there waiting, apparently, for the key to turn in the lock once more. Nothing that I had imagined would happen took place; and what I had thought was no more than a nightmare that caused Jane to wake suddenly in the night, as we lay entwined in the narrow bed she believed would be exchanged for a four-poster, once she and Papa were back from their long honeymoon in Europe, turned out to be a prefiguration of the truth.

I went to the wedding, whether I was wanted there or not, as Jane only laughed away my attempts to inform her of the imminent arrival of the great Céline Varens at

Thornfield Hall and insisted on donning her bridal attire and setting off down the drive with Monsieur Rochester, to celebrate their nuptials. I it was, therefore, who saw the two strangers as they lingered in the little churchyard before going into the church; and I alone, creeping in behind them and well concealed by the tall, carved pew at the back of the aisle, was able to witness the preparations of the more sallow-faced of the two men who had come so quietly into the building. Holding up his hand at the point in the service when the clergyman, looking around and asking if there was any reason Papa and Jane should not wed, this man who looked familiar (I felt I had seen him with Grace perhaps, on the third story of the house at one time), this stranger announced in a loud voice that there was indeed a reason this *mariage* could not take place. Papa had a "wife living," at Thornfield Hall. The stranger did not speak of Maman at all, and of the fact that a child born to parents constitutes a *mariage* already between them. And Monsieur Rochester turned and began to shout, as if he knew that the small congregation would be deaf to what he had to say.

Now I understand that the strange

woman who was my Antoinette has altered beyond recognition because she realized that Papa was in love with another, and she would no longer be Papa's wife. And now I am back from the church and the fiasco of the wedding that never took place, and I have turned the key in the lock of my room, so I have made myself a prisoner, like the woman Papa married in the unimaginable years before I was born.

The sky grew dark, and the night that followed the day that was to have been the great occasion for Miss Eyre was hard to tell apart from the preceding hours of afternoon and evening. I stayed in my room, imagining poor Bertha/Antoinette in her cell once more — yet I could feel no pity for her, only revulsion. Was this woman, who had walked across the park with me as if we had never once met in our lives, the bride Papa had brought from the West Indies, as big and clumsy and brightly colored as the moth that flies on summer nights into the candles at Thornfield? Did he love her, as once he had loved Maman? It was impossible to believe.

Jane stayed in her room also, and for her I felt as little compassion as I did for the madwoman on the upper floor of

Thornfield Hall. She must weep, I knew, but the disastrous consequences of her attempt to take Papa from Maman and myself filled me merely with a cool pleasure. That I must act soon and execute the plan I had formed became clear to me on the evening of the second day, when, trying to keep up a pretense of life going on as normal in the house, Madame Fairfax informed me we should have tea in the library, this as always a precinct of Monsieur Rochester and guarded fiercely by Pilot, the only member of the household to appear unaltered by the dramatic turn of events at the church the previous day. I was told to put on my plaid dress — there was no mention of Papa's change of direction and his decision to stay at Thornfield rather than go off across Europe on his *lune de miel* with a bride who could not be his — and Madame F herself brushed my hair and fixed my ringlets, as Leah, along with some other members of the staff, had mysteriously disappeared.

Jane Eyre left the house just after midnight. Outside my door she paused, and I heard her catch her breath and sigh. That she had had affection for me, I cannot gainsay; but I had been for her a conduit to the greater profit of her master's love, and little more. I could fancy her delight at hearing, had she and Monsieur Rochester wed unlawfully and gone to the white villa (Maman's house, as I well know), of the fruitless journey of Céline Varens to Thornfield Hall, to find her bridegroom flown and the house she had thought to share with him empty and deserted. If Miss Eyre had met Maman, I have no doubt she would have shown respect for her, though she considers herself a moral being far above one who acts and dances for a living. But, Miss Eyre, you are returned to a miserable governess in urgent need of employment now!

However, by the time remorse at my uncharitable thoughts had led me to unlock my bedroom door and peer out into the dark corridor, Jane Eyre had gone.

Eleven

Adèle

It was not difficult to gain access to the attic, as Grace Poole was not only drunk but actually insensible on the floor. I had to wake her, and I tried to persuade Grace, bribing her with the last of the money Jenny had given me, to tell me more of her wretched charge's whereabouts. For the cell door was swinging open — and the strange woman was nowhere to be seen.

It was just as I thought: those who wish to fly away have only one idea, at Thornfield; and Grace, who has no head for heights, refused to accompany me to the small staircase with the window that opens out onto the roof. Only Mrs. Fairfax — I had been into the housekeeper's room barely half an hour earlier; she had brushed out my hair and given me a mug of the sweet pink tea as a reward for putting up with the pain of the fifty brush-strokes and ensuing agony of ringlets — was bustling along the top passage of the house with a pile of starched pillowcases and the like, saw me, and said sharply that there'd be trouble in store if I started mucking about on the roof again. But I dodged past her and went ahead all the same. Once there, I gazed once more with pride at the cannon up there on the highest roof, trained on any enemy of our master, Papa! And I reflected that I was still so proud of him, so desirous to end the impediment to happiness in his life and from which he, like the foolish Creole he had married, had no notion how to escape. Maman would come and marry Papa as soon as it was known that *la pauvre* Antoinette was dead. Of this I was certain, as I stood by the highest turret, gazing down on all Yorkshire laid out before me.

It was some time before I saw her. She did not move — but she was not a dead body yet. A living woman, very weak and frightened, she clung to a stone balustrade just below me and almost sobbed with relief at the sight of me as I stepped out of the window onto the only flat portion of the roof.

"Why are you so long coming to me, child?" the crazy woman gasped. Her face was very shrunken and thin, and I saw that the *folle* must have wandered away again from her drunken warder as soon as we were back at Thornfield. By the look of her, she could have been two days out on the roof without food or water. She was trapped — no doubt she had been trying, as only a madwoman would, to climb down the front of the house and reach the ground — and I saw that her hands were bloodstained from clinging to the parapet and that her strength was nearly gone. Ah, if only I could return to this moment, if I could replay this scene, as I found it to be, for I had no feeling in my heart for Antoinette any longer, and my sensations belonged more to the theater than to real life. As I stood there, on the narrow sill that divided the *pauvre folle* from a return to her past existence at Thornfield Hall and a certain death on the cobbles of the courtyard below, I struggled, I know, to recover those human affections I had once had for my French captive, the mother who called me *doudou* even if she came from an island far away. But, as I tried to show a human concern, the colors and shapes of the passage, the window, and the roof outside all changed; the distance between myself and Antoinette turned into an unbridgeable gulf; and a cloud as long and black as a whale settled ominously in the sky outside.

171

"Come to me, child!" I hear still her piteous wails as I stepped back inside the window, brought it down behind me, and stepped from the sill onto the narrow stair. By a stroke of ill fortune, Madame F came pounding along again, this time with a pair of curtains washed and ready for hanging. So I hid, on the ledge by the boxroom with the square door where Antoinette and I had played when we were friends.

And I could hear La Fairfax as she poked about on the turret stair, looking for me. Then, tut-tutting with impatience, she walked on.

It was not long before I knew there were other, pressing reasons Maman must come, and quickly, if Papa was to be saved from the possibility of a life of insufferable boredom with the governess, Miss Eyre. For I feared that Jane would return, drawn by his promises of the white villa and by the certainty of Papa's love for her. I shuddered when I remembered Madame Fairfax's words: "She will be like a sister to you," the housekeeper had said, and I pray each moment this "sister" will not come.

On the day this gray mouse came into the house that is Papa's and mine, everything changed in the story, like the pantomime of *Cinderella* when Cinders arrives at the ball and the handsome prince falls in love with her. Sometimes in those days at Thornfield Hall I felt as if I were watching a pantomime from *le paradis*, my seat up in the gods, the highest place in the theater, where my lovely Pierrot kept me smiling through all those dark afternoons when Maman was too preoccupied with her new role to take me in her arms. Jane Eyre and Papa! This was a masquerade that I could only be dreaming. And I heard the voice of Félix, as he tried to comfort me.

"Adèle, this dull little person will go away soon," he said when he came to me in my dreams, on the days Jane would insist I finish my lessons instead of going into town where Madame Potts the milliner lived, who said she could make me a new bonnet in time for Easter day. I remembered Félix taking me to the fair of the *pain d'épice* — I could taste the spiced bread when I woke — so as to think as little as possible of our schoolroom meals of boiled mutton and cabbage and tapioca pudding that Madame F will not permit me to refuse. Félix would tell me to run away from Thornfield and return to him in his studio. But then Jenny — Jenny holding the whip Maman inherited from her circus days — would come and lock me in a dreadful little room in her *appartement,* and my heart began to beat fast before I woke up. There was no escape here, from Madame F and Jane Eyre day after day.

I soon discovered that Papa had fallen for the lures of the little gray mouse, my governess, Jane. If he was bad-tempered, she learned to stand up to him — that was her trick, and from the first it went very well with a *grand seigneur* like Monsieur Rochester, who is accustomed to being obeyed whatever he may ask of people. The very first time she and I were summoned to the library, I was dismissed without even trying on the robe of organdy with the beautiful flowers embroidered along the hem — a dress Papa could have found only in Paris, so my eyes filled with tears of hope that he had gone there in search of Maman. "Run upstairs, Adèle," said Miss Eyre, as if she were the one accustomed to giving orders here, not Papa. And I saw him look at her admiringly — oh, he liked the voice of command. I remember, when I used to hide myself on the top step of the grand staircase from the hall in rue Vaugirard, that I would hear Maman speak to him like that — when he was still the milord stranger. Then there would come the crack of the whip. But this would cause Jenny, if she came in just then, to bundle me off to bed as furious as I ever saw her, when she was looking after Maman.

I cannot think of these things without sorrow, but I hear the voices and I know I am an actress, and one day I will walk on the stage and speak in a voice no one can fail to respect. For now I have to try to forget scenes such as this one: Papa is down in the grand salon, explaining to the little governess that it is he who gives the orders here at Thornfield. "Go in there, do that," and so on. And he laughs. He asks Miss Eyre if she can play the piano, and she says, "A little," and he teases her. "The expected answer," says Papa — and from where I sit, in the highest seat here on the stairs at Thornfield, I see him as he comes half out into the hall as if to check that I am really gone. Then he closes the dark mahogany double doors. One thing is also true, however: Papa's face is quite different now from the picture on the plate Félix made that day in Paris before putting it onto paper and placing it in my hand. The face I carried that day of the fair of the *pain d'épice* — the hard rectangle of card that chafed my skin through the pocket of my pantalettes — had an expression Papa no longer wears since Jane Eyre came to Thornfield Hall.

So this was how I knew before anyone that Jane — no sister of mine, however she might try to win the affection of her "dear Adèle" — would win the love of the man I knew must love no one but Maman and me.

Maman will come to Thornfield Hall; I cannot believe the words of the drunken woman who kept Papa's first wife under lock and key. Maman will never forget her love for Papa or for her darling daughter, little Adèle.

As I wait behind the locked door of my room to learn my fate — now that Jane has gone, am I banished from Thornfield? where will Papa go? — I hear in memory his voice and Jane's together. And I go to the window, to look out as the summer evening draws in and shadows lengthen on the walls.

"Jane." I am already dressed and running through the Hall to find Madame Fairfax for tea when I hear the voice of Monsieur Rochester in the inner drawing room, the room where the governess used to play her abysmal nocturnes and waltzes and Papa sat there with a foolish smile on his face as he listened to her. Now there is no music: only the sound of sobbing, sometimes hers and even, I believe, also his. Then, "I only ask you to endure one more night under this roof, Jane, and then farewell to its miseries and terrors forever! I have a place to repair to, which will be a secure sanctuary from hateful reminiscences, from unwelcome intrusion — even from falsehood and slander."

"And take Adèle with you, sir," comes Jane's voice out to me by the chest in the hall. "She will be a companion for you."

"What do you mean, Jane? I told you I would send Adèle to school. And what do I want with a child for a companion, and not my own child — a French dancer's bastard? Why do you assign Adèle to me for a companion?"

I did not move from my place on the Hall floor, half hidden by the old Chinese chest John walks around each day, to beat the gong at mealtimes. Yet I must have shifted against it, for a muffled note came from the great brass circle in its ornate frame. I could not move; it was the voices that moved, up and down the scale of passion and sorrow, such as I had never heard from a woman and a man before. Always, it seemed, the governess held out in the face of all Papa's offers and pleas for her to

177

stay with him. If I could hate her for it, then I would: so I thought as I knelt on that hard floor, turned to stone. But there was too much to admire in her intransigence — until I could feel only praise in my heart for her after all. I could only admire her, even though Papa would deny that I am his child. "You shall be Mrs. Rochester," he is saying to Jane, "both virtually and nominally I shall keep only to you as long as you and I live. You shall go to a place I have in the South of France: a whitewashed villa on the shores of the Mediterranean. There you shall live a happy, and guarded, and most innocent life. . . ."

I waited only long enough to hear the refusal on Jane's part. I knew that she would flee Thornfield; I heard the anger and sadness in my father's voice as she turned down even the white villa by the sea.

There was no sensation in me, neither love nor hate. I returned to my room and awaited the day when I would be banished from my rightful home. Yet I refused at the same time to believe my fate. How could I be put to school when Maman would appear any moment now, as in a bold new pantomime, and claim Papa for her own?

One week after Jane Eyre left Thornfield

Hall, John the footman accompanied me in the coach that took me away to school, and only Madame Fairfax waved good-bye to me on the step. Papa sat morosely in his study. All the servants, with the exception of John and Mary — and Grace Poole, who stayed on the upper floor with her gin and porter — were gone. My father has not written to me, nor has it occurred to him that I am truly an orphan here, without father or mother to give me a place in the world. I think with an affection I never knew I had of Jane Eyre from time to time, although, *naturellement*, it was a great mistake on her part to think she could marry Papa. Madame F has come to visit me a few times, the last occasion being a week or so ago. "You're thin and pale, Adèle," said the kind old lady, and she brought sweetmeats and other trifles from her bag, as well as her famous rose hips, to make an infusion, which I have done. Leah, who works in the milliner's at Millcote, sent a note to me at school — this written for her — saying there is no sign of Miss Eyre's returning to Thornfield. The governess hasn't been seen since the day she walked up the aisle of Thornfield Church and came down it again as much a spinster as the day she was born.

If I act now, I shall have Papa at last. We shall wait for Maman together.

It is summer again, the month I began my perilous journey from Paris, exactly a year ago. It is July in this dark place with the gray wooden floors that are wet each morning from water and carbolic soap, this place that smells of cabbage and sadness and from which the inmates never can escape. The place where Papa sent me so I could learn I must not trust in his love, is Hatherleigh School, and I have waited only for the first rays of the summer sun to make my way back to him. This time, however he may try to deceive me, I shall show Papa that I know he loves me. I shall care for him for the rest of his days. And I shall also let him know his secret is safe with me: I have visited the chamber, and I hold the key.

I had not been long at Thornfield Hall when I found that Leah, the maid, would encourage me in my attempts to fasten my circus wings and fly, dangerous though this undoubtedly was. Perhaps already the servants at Thornfield knew I was of little value to their master and did not figure in his plans.

I left the school quite easily by way of

going high on the roof and sailing down on my circus wings. These, gifts from a long-gone life, from Pierrot, who always saw when I was sad or lonesome at Maman's lengthy absences from me on the boards, have saved me often enough before — they led me to the battlements of Thornfield, after all, and to the discovery of poor mad Antoinette — and if I had not lost all the love for her that had once been in me, on the day she fell to her death, Papa would be burdened with her still.

To reach Thornfield I took the coach, which set me down at Whitcross; and I ran up the long lime drive to the house. Mrs. Fairfax was there to admit me; she had written to me of the day she intended to return to Thornfield to collect her belongings (for, as it transpired, Papa had emptied the house of most of the staff after Jane left and I was sent away to school), and I tricked the good housekeeper into believing I wished only to find my favorite toy, Punchinello, and so would go straight to my room. But I went around to the French window in the west wing, and I ran still, this time up and up, higher and higher, to the attic where Grace would sit, head in hand, by her bottle of gin. But there's no sign of her here now.

The sun comes in the small window in the eaves. I take the magnifying glass from its bag on my arm, and hold it under the strong rays of the July sun, training it directly on a paper fan — a pretty thing, it must have belonged to the crazy woman once — that lies on Grace's table.

The flames start small, like Félix's miniature fireworks, set off to keep me happy in the long hours while he develops his pictures in his studio. Then they grow; and to save my life I run: down and down, for there is no time to take out and attach my wings. How can fire make walls, as this one does? The voice of La Cibot sounds in my ears: "Fire loves you, Adèle." And I know I must take with me the picture of Papa in my room and rush in there through the flames and pull out a stool to fetch it from the top of the chest of drawers . . . and then, as the fire closes around me on the crashing stairs, I leap from the turret window . . . and fly. . . .

Part Two

Twelve

Edward

It is five years since Thornfield Hall was re-built, after a fire that started up in the attics succeeded in burning a great part of the house to the ground. In the ensuing chaos I, Edward Rochester, was blinded and maimed, and little Adèle, who had been un-expectedly visiting Thornfield on that day, was found unconscious in the parterre where she had fallen from a high story. God gives me guidance to thank Him for her re-covery from the effects of this tragic disaster, in which it was reported that Bertha Mason leaped to her death in an attempt to evade the conflagration.

They were alike, the wretched Creole and the *fillette* who demanded of me that I love her as a father: they craved a man to lead them, and they had no spirit of their own, neither pride nor independence in a world they saw as belonging precisely to the paternal figures they have been denied. And so they were vengeful! Had they understood my Jane, so resolute, proud, and fine, they would have seen a life without misery and madness; as it is, poor Antoinette lost her life without coming to understand the qualities of the woman who is now my loving wife.

There are other reasons for my sad, reflective state of mind at present. Adèle leaves school today to come to us, to be greeted by Jane, the guiding spirit of her young years. Adèle never to my knowledge obeyed her governess, preferring to mock and jeer and make up to me with all the skills of her own mother, a *courtisane*. Could she not see that Jane had merely a desire to assist a child reared without morality? That the rules of Paris are not played here in England, and certainly not here in the north — where once I knew misery and feared for my own mind — before Jane returned to me, bringing happiness and calm.

This state of marital harmony must continue, and Jane must never learn of my suspicion that her "little Adèle" escaped on the day of the fire from the school to which she had been sent, and came here to try to claim a paternal affection from me. Jane, mother of my son and heavy now with our second child, will give as much as she is

186

able to the daughter I cannot publicly accept as mine, for all the "proof" that has come from France in these past years (not from Céline; she has too much cunning for direct communication) from Jenny Colon, a woman whose tone — self-justifying, masculine, intolerable — I abhor. My cherished young wife trusts me to instill in Adèle, after five years of the new boarding school I instructed should be as strict as possible, a belief in Christian values along with a love of this country, which is in all probability still as appealing to the child as the bowl of cold porridge they have required her to eat daily in the seminary. She must learn, as I have, to like the days that pass here. As my sight returns to me, I recognize and salute the sky of steel, the sternness and stillness of this landscape, winter and summer both. I like Thornfield: its old crow trees and thorn trees; its gray façade and lines of dark windows. All that Adèle — and the poor insane Antoinette before her — loathed to the very core of her being, feeling the prison of my refusal to love her — but how could I? how could I? — the child must now learn to give grateful thanks for. I welcome back each day with the blessed growing sharpness of my eyes.

I admit that the curbing of my natural instincts is proving harder than poor Jane had hoped. I hate still; I act with speed against my enemy; I suffer, most of all, from the sin of despair. (But who can reproach me, victim first of an avaricious father and then of a mad wife?) My house has been burned, I have been blinded and maimed: surely, as the good Lord revives in me the greatest of his gifts, that of vision, I must lose my vices and dedicate myself in true humility to a lease of life I had long thought could never be mine. Have I not done penance enough, for committing the mortal sin of murder, when I took the life of Céline's lover? Am I not fully aware of the suffering inflicted on the women who loved me? Now I am saved — by the elfin creature who first startled me on horseback here at the gates to Thornfield — she who could have followed God and wed the missionary of whom she still speaks some nights in her sleep — rescued from the pit of eternal misery by my darling Jane. Surely I can find peace of mind at last?

But I confess it comes slowly, this calm and contentment of which philosophers and God-fearing men speak. On some days, it's true, I sense the wind as it blows on the moor, and all the living, hidden creatures that breathe beneath the ling and gorse: my heart is filled with the glory of Creation.

On other days I could wish myself a supplicant in the Romish church, so deep is the abyss created by my misdeeds, my cruelties, the pain my power here and abroad has led me to commit. I would kneel by a curtained box — like my father and his before him I disdain the papists and their idolatry, but now I am led to wonder if they are not the true followers of Jesus Christ — and I would pour my heart out to a man I cannot see.

Is this what it has come to? Can I never make amends? Jane will not support my black moods, as she calls them in that light, quiet voice of hers, which would blow them out onto the moor as surely as the northeasterly that comes today to chase my horrors away. "Edward, none of us is without sin," she says, looking at me profoundly, but with a smile half etched on the small mouth whose dictates I followed so long when quite blind. "Take little Edward and walk up to the kitchen garden with him. Show him what grows there, even in the hardest winter: how the snowdrop and the willow are pushing through."

I take the child on these occasions, and the miracle of life restores me, as the infant stares in wonder at the snowdrop, first herald of the spring. In summer I take the child to the hothouse, and peach juice dribbles down his chin as he cries out in delight. And I can see him more clearly, day by day! My wife, by bearing another child, demonstrates her belief in me, in Thornfield, in a future without pain or strife.

But on some days I am no sooner in my study, in the house I have built up again from the ashes of the past, than I am plunged into darkness once more. I see Antoinette, in the hammock on the veranda of the accursed place where the birds that were like tropical crows, with their insistent, metallic call, mocked her mad eyes and my own breaking heart. I see the journey back to England: her bafflement at the cold, lightless sky; the good days when she danced and pirouetted on the lawn here — and the gradual, ghastly descent as she lost her mind. And then I wander further, retracing the steps that led the "milord" to France and Germany and Italy, in search of recompense for a bargain struck in the infernal regions. How they loved my gold, these women I picked and left, discarded as soon as outworn. How gold, which formed the basis of my father's hellish pact, was what attracted them! — this is the thought I have. And then, too frequently and with knowledge of a burden of remorse and shame, I think of Céline Varens. Even to Jane I have painted her as a mercenary pest, a woman who lived solely to scratch the fortunes from her lovers' adoration, their disillusion growing as she emptied their purses and ran away.

But it was not so. Céline lived for the high wire, she walked across the highest span of the Funambules without support or fear. She knew herself a great actress — but who would give a circus high-wire dancer the chance to play Racine or Corneille? She was marooned in her acrobat's costume, chained to the horse she rode standing bareback in her tinsel pantaloons cut off high above the knee. I offered her the path — with my gold, it is true — to study with the great, to turn from entertainer to tragedienne. And just as she began to train her voice and learn the lineaments of true passion, I threw her from her house and home for the venial sin of spending a day at the races with a young fop whom I knew in my heart she took to seeing when I was away — and in whom she had no true interest.

Céline, where are you now? Wandering in Italy still with a vagrant musician who has neither understanding nor appreciation of your talents? Accept my appeal for pardon — even if I did not love you with sufficient selflessness, I should not have treated you in this way. If you come here — and one day you will perhaps seek your daughter and mine in this bare moorland country — you will witness my remorse for my past treatment of you. You will see the meaning of true love, when you witness my Jane and the man you once placed on a pinnacle, for respecting your wish to become a true actress. "You are not like most men," Céline said; it was a cool day, and we rested indoors, in our white villa where mimosa trees grow, by the sea. "You care for my soul, and you know I aim high," she said, and I hear her words now and shudder at my vile indifference to her, on the occasion I decided to punish her infidelity to me.

It is time for me to find Jane; and on days such as this I find her one hundred times in a single morning — a result, possibly, of the dependence I had on her for three long years after we first wed. There are other reasons, also, for my need of dear

Jane. She will banish my thoughts — of Antoinette, of Céline, of the other women I tortured with false promises of love and enduring happiness. We shall walk together — she slowly, mindful of the child she brings to the eighth month — to the lake, to the new staircase of water constructed at the far end by the chestnut tree, which will fulfill her dreams as it descends in rivulets of music all night long. Jane will turn to me and say she hopes for a daughter, for we already have a son —

There. As I go out onto the terrace from my study and walk down the stone steps to the parterre, I see a figure by the wicket gate that leads out onto the moor.

She is beautiful — even more beautiful than I remember her. A face that is a heart lit by pools of dancing brown water under straight brows. Ringlets, black as night, gathered at the nape of a neck I can taste and smell, so strongly does it come back to me.

Céline — but it is not she. This young woman, who looks back at me with the frank, fearless gaze of Céline Varens, tosses her head as her lost mother once had done, and she smiles, the child I once knew as Adèle. Now this apparition will come in. A slender hand at the latch to open the gate and bring her here. . . .

And as I call Adèle's name, Jane appears from the study's French window, her gaze following my trajectory of a mere few seconds before, running down the flight of steps to my side.

Jane sees no one there, at the side of the lichen-covered gate under the dark-laden branches of an Irish yew. She gazes at me anxiously — for she fears for my eyesight, and any mistaken vision bodes ill for the coming days.

I look again, and there is indeed no one there. With my dear wife I walk down to inspect the improvements in the gardens of Thornfield Hall.

Thirteen

Mrs. Fairfax

It was something in the region of two months after the little governess packed her bags and left Thornfield Hall, her hopes and happiness destroyed, that Mr. Edward Fairfax Rochester came up to inform me I must go, too, to cousins in the remote north of Scotland, an island, to be precise, and not a spot I would have chosen for myself in the circumstances. For, as I had expected, it grows dark at noon on the bare outcrop of rock that is the home of Lord and Lady Doune, and however much I put in in the mornings, in the way of patching linens and cleaning silver sadly left to rust in the damp Atlantic air, night invariably descends before I complete my task, and the remainder of the day must be spent knitting garments too simple to require a pattern.

It was at Inchalan Island, therefore, that I heard news of the burning of Thornfield Hall; and Lord Doune's demeanor was very grave when he summoned me out from the downstairs housekeeper's sitting room of the ancient keep that is his ancestral home and requested me to take a seat in the old arbor, protected from the gales that blow in night and day there. "Cousin Fairfax," says His Lordship, "I have shocking news for you." And he proceeded to recount the story I have heard so many times since, after returning to Thornfield at Mr. Rochester's sudden instruction. The accounts do not vary overmuch. Fire broke out as it was growing dark, and flames spread throughout the house before engines could arrive from Millcote. A great proportion of the valuable antique furniture was destroyed inside the house, and the fire took hold so rapidly on the ground and first floors that Mr. Rochester was hard-pressed to run to the attics — but this he had done. "And what did Cousin Edward hope to find there?" I asked Lord Doune, for I have learned in life that to assume innocence of even the most basic facts brings greater reward than the demonstration of a knowledge of events.

"It was said that Edward Rochester had a lunatic wife living up there," replied Lord Doune when a brief silence between us had passed. "We had — along with everyone else — assumed him to be unmarried. And yet despite the existence of a wife living, our kinsman had wished to marry a young woman, a Miss —"

"Eyre," I said.

"Yes, you must have had more than a superficial acquaintance with her," said my host and employer, refraining, however, from meeting my eye and gazing instead out at the limitless gray sea that stretches, so he has informed me, all the way to America. "No doubt Edward was wrong to contemplate bigamy, as he did, though his situation must, even to elders of the church in these islands, be demanding of sympathy. The tragic part, so I believe, is that Rochester came too late to the battlements, and his wife threw herself off."

"And how did you hear that, sir?" I asked. Something in Lord Doune's words and manner of expressing himself had me wondering at the identity of the bearer of the tale. For I knew better than anyone else that poor Mr. Rochester's insane wife had been disposed of in quite a different way, and a good time before the fire of which I had just been told.

"I could not expect Edward to write to me directly," came the prompt and truthful answer. "He has lost his true home, and I am informed that he is cared for at

Ferndean Manor, somewhere on the estate." Lord Doune must have seen me shudder, for he paused again; and as we both stood quietly looking out to sea, I thought of the conversations on the subject of an impending influx of visitors I had had with my master, these being the sole occasions when the possibility would arise of his admitting to the existence of a person living but hidden in the uppermost extremities of the Hall. "Mrs. Fairfax, I may require you to ready Ferndean Manor for a new occupant," Mr. Rochester had said to me two or three times (this before the arrival of Miss Eyre, it must be stated: the requests would usually coincide with the imminent visit of Miss Ingram and her mother, Lady Ingram). And, as I recall so well, my reply was invariably the same, to wit that the manor was famously damp and would need months and not days of fires and airing to prepare it for human habitation. I never, in the course of these exchanges, showed the slightest curiosity as to why Mr. Rochester made these demands; and indeed, before long, they were referred to between us as emergency measures, in the event Lady Ingram brought a greater retinue than had been expected. I always knew that my employer was aware he could count on my discretion in this, as in all else concerning his private arrangements.

Lord Doune was silent a while longer; then His Lordship went on to tell me — and deeply saddened I was to hear it — that my master had, either permanently or temporarily, been blinded by the fire at Thornfield and had been maimed also, whether in his right or left arm had not been made clear. The landlord of the inn not far from Millcote — a mere two miles across fields from the Hall — was, it transpired, an Archie Campbell, who had previously served Lord and Lady Doune at Inchalan — and it was from his pen that these pieces of information flowed. He had some of the facts right, I supposed, but I was wary of believing the entire account. To test my host, and without his knowing I was doing so, I proceeded to inquire as to the manner of the "madwoman's" conduct, once Mr. Rochester had arrived too late on the battlements to save her. Had she turned, as lunatics will, on her husband, despite the grave danger in which they found themselves? How, in short, had the ghastly scene begun and ended?

"Cousin Edward went back to get his mad wife out of her cell," said the master of Inchalan somberly. "And then they — the servants, that is, and Archie Campbell himself, who had seen the blaze from the inn and rushed across the fields — called out to him that she was on the roof, where she was standing, waving her arms above the battlements, and shouting out till they could hear her a mile off. Campbell saw her and heard her with his own eyes. Several onlookers witnessed Mr. Rochester ascend through the skylight onto the roof; they heard him call 'Bertha!' They saw him approach her; and then, madam, she yelled, and gave a spring, and the next minute she lay smashed on the pavement. So badly smashed, they say, there was nothing left of her face — so there was no knowing what manner of woman she was."

"Dead?" I said, and Lord Doune nodded before the word was out of my mouth. "I see," I said, with as much an air of grief as the sad tale demanded. "This is a dreadful happening, my lord, and I know you will respect my greater sense of duty to Mr. Rochester, should he be in need of my services in his new and drastically altered situation. I am as well aware of the drawbacks attached to living at Ferndean Manor, especially in winter, as anyone; and if the master has John and Mary caring for him there, I shall be glad to direct them."

Lord Doune replied that he understood perfectly and that he would forward any command from Mr. Rochester to me without delay. This, however, took some time to come, as I have already explained, and in the meanwhile various thoughts and memories came to me that I kept to myself, despite the curiosity shown by Janet, the maid at Inchalan, a sister and therefore confidante of the landlord of the inn at Millcote, Archie Campbell. I needed time, I knew, to examine the evidence sent north by the host of the Rochester Arms, before coming to my own conclusions. But the account I was given, as I know, is not accurate. And it soon became clear to me that my hosts and employers wished keenly to learn the facts of the tragedy at Thornfield Hall.

"Come in, Mrs. Fairfax, and sit down." Thus was I summoned by Lady Doune to give an account of the time I had passed at Thornfield before coming north to the islands of the Hebrides, to act as housekeeper to the noble kinsfolk of my relative, Edward Rochester. That I had been asked nothing — or very little, at least — on the subject of the setup at the Hall since my arrival at the castle, I had put down to the reasonable assumption by my employers that I would have little to tell. Mr. Rochester, a bachelor with a known appetite for traveling abroad, had been rumored long enough to be about to become engaged to Miss Blanche Ingram to have stopped being an item of interest, to kin or acquaintance alike. He was an unmarried man; tales of the extent of his fortune varied considerably (this I knew from the inadvertent overhearing of conversations in the drawing room, before the ladies went up to change); and the general opinion of my excellent master was of a man who was the prototype of a bachelor: interested in the running of his estate, keen to marry when the time came and raise a family, and not hurried in any of his ways. Now there came a story of fire, followed by madness and possible murder or suicide. Lady Doune placed me very tenderly in a low, needlework-covered chair in her boudoir and proceeded to demand I "fill in the gaps," as she very succinctly termed it.

"So, my dear Mrs. Fairfax, tell me about the governess our cousin wished to make his wife. Unlawfully, we hear. Is this correct? Did Mr. Rochester, up until the time of the fire at his house, have a wife living there, unknown to everybody?"

"Lady Doune," I replied, "there is nought, as we both know well, that servants and keepers of hostelries like better than to invent and fabricate the most lurid of tales when misfortune strikes at their betters. Edward Rochester did not have a wife living at Thornfield Hall, to my knowledge; but he was a man of tested loyalties and never dismissed anyone from his service, even if they fell fatally ill or went so far as to lose their reason."

As I spoke these words, I knew them to be the gospel truth, so help me God. Not once in all the long years I passed at Thornfield Hall did I gain a glimpse of the "ghost," as Leah and some of the foolish maids called the vision they claimed would pass sometimes down the stone spiral staircase and emerge on the second-story landing of Thornfield Hall. Rumors and hearsay are one thing, evidence of one's own eyes another. "There is neither ghost nor wife at Thornfield," said I as Lady Doune sat staring at me in much the same way her husband had done.

"How do you explain the fact the wedding between Mr. Rochester and Miss Eyre was stopped?" persisted Lady Doune. "If there had not been an impediment to the marriage, would not the ceremony have taken place?"

I confess I have thought long on the subject of my master's matrimonial intentions — with Miss Blanche Ingram, with Miss Eyre, and even with the mother of the little French girl, who lived under the impression, poor child, that her "Céline Varens" would arrive any day to wed the man she called Papa, whether he be such or not. So great was the child's ability to deceive herself on the subject of her mother's coming that she addressed letters to herself from the absent mother, these discovered by Leah in the fork of a tree and brought to me. I attempted to explain to Her Ladyship that our mutual cousin, for all his excellent qualities, was congenitally unable to decide on a bride, a future chatelaine of the Hall. "He would announce his engagement and then call it off," I said. "He rigged it up, very probably, that two strangers would appear and show 'proof' of Mr. Rochester's previous tie. It worked well: the service was called off, and the intended wife of Mr. Rochester left the house the very next day."

"Odd indeed," mused Lady Doune. "Why did he not marry Blanche Ingram, then?" she went on with a sharper tone.

"My lady, we all expected it," said I. "The family diamonds were sent up by the bank from London — and these I saw with my own eyes. The engagement dinner was on two occasions planned and then called off. John the butler can give you more details — there are so many, regarding the postponed or canceled betrothals of Edward Rochester."

"So who was it who put it about that Edward Rochester had a wife already living at the time of the fire, by those who did not know the facts?" asked Lady Doune, her voice and expression showing extreme uncertainty as to what or whom she might next believe. My answer, however, convinced the good countess, I am reasonably sure, of the truth of my words.

"Why, the woman who spread this calumny was an old housemaid, my lady, who had long ago succumbed to the temptations of alcohol; and while indulging herself in her master's cellar, had lost her sanity along with any sobriety or good judgment she might once have possessed."

"Good heavens!" exclaimed Lady Doune.

"I warned Miss Eyre," I continued, "the new governess come to the Hall to teach the French ward — or daughter — of Mr.

Rochester, to pay scant attention to the laughter and menacing sounds she heard soon after her arrival there. They emanated from Grace Poole — that was the woman's name."

"The child was — is — Edward's daughter?" gasped the noblewoman. "I was informed the child was adopted, when Archie Campbell wrote to us from the inn at Millcote."

"Indeed, she is both," I replied. "Little Adela was convinced that the promises made by her 'Papa' to the dancer in Paris who is the child's mother would be honored, and shortly. These were promises of marriage, most certainly."

"I am astonished," Lady Doune confessed in a faint voice.

Lady Doune was able, when I had done, to inform me that she now understood fully the illusion all those at Thornfield labor under, who believed that a "madwoman" perished in the flames at Thornfield. Her cousin Edward Rochester would certainly have run up to the roof, to try to ascertain the extent of damage already caused by the fire. The drunken servant — Grace Poole — it must have been who leaped to her death and was disfigured beyond recognition. I agreed heartily with this and, when pressed, replied that of any other victim of the blaze at Thornfield I know nought. But I kept for myself one certain resolution: should the governess or the French child, now safely locked away at school, come to the Hall again when I am there (and surely I will be), then they must suffer for their innocence. For I fear for my master's life, if the truth should finally come out one day.

Fourteen

Edward

I confess that it is hard, from time to time, to be married to a strong woman. My Jane, who has all the probity and endurance that is to be expected from one who has transformed from a slip of a girl, an orphan, to governess in a household distinctly unlike those to which her school companions would have been dispatched once sufficiently armed with knowledge — has suffered many experiences already, at the age of twenty-three, and yet shows neither cynicism nor an awareness of limited expectations as a result of them. Has not Jane refused a man of God, a missionary, in order to be with her Edward? Did she not traverse the moors in obedience to a call not spoken but heard in the human heart? Do I not owe everything to Jane? Yet this sense of obligation has come to hobble me, when the moral rights and wrongs of any situation are put to me, by the one I love. Her unflinching response to the demands of duty — as she sees them — demands in turn from me a dedication I cannot on each occasion supply. Can the child bride and Edward not be happy together, without sacrificing the tranquillity so dearly won? We have a son and await another child. Is it right in the eyes of God that our family should now extend to receive one who must by this time be little more than a stranger?

For Jane it is who insists that young Adèle be released from the school she has attended for five years, and come to live with us at Thornfield. As if guided by an instinct I had not known I possessed, I found I was subjected to a vision of the child's mother, Céline, standing at the wicket gate in the lower part of the garden, only yesterday. The minx — whom I realised, if she was, as Adèle, playing tricks on me still — stared me full in the face and then walked on, to disappear on the Millcote road. But this I could not, naturally, confide to Jane — who must consider me rid of any thoughts concerning Céline Varens. The matter disturbed me, I admit: was this apparition a warning against refusing a home and protection to the child? Or was it, as I am bound to believe, a prophecy of the doom that will descend once more on Thornfield Hall if she is admitted? It is unlike me to remain silent, I am aware, when domestic problems are aired by the young Jane Rochester; but we are close enough, my darling and I, to find a solution to this most difficult of dilemmas, that concerning the welcoming of a child who may or may not be mine into the bosom of the family.

"It is of no consequence to me," Jane remarked as we sit, this lovely May morning, on the new ornamental seat in the bower built around the split chestnut tree by the sunken fence in the garden. (Here, for perhaps a good reason, we choose to go when we have matters to fight over: the lightning-struck tree brings back to us the fateful night of my proposal to a trembling little Jane Eyre.) "It is of no great import to me, Edward, whether Adèle is truly your daughter or not," continued Jane. "She is the child I came to Thornfield to teach; she is my reason for being here and for loving you."

"Jane — come here." I try, when my sweet wife speaks such endearments to me, to catch her in my arms and change the subject, so we are in harmony all day long. But today, as ever, my strong little spouse would have none of it. "Edward, I gave my promises to Adèle when she knew nothing of right or wrong, her upbringing having denied her even the most basic tenets of belief in God. How much does she need us both now that she is close to fourteen years old? If we abandon her at this time, once having shown fidelity and affection to the child, is this not worse than leaving her in the gutter where her mother expected her to dance like an organ grinder's monkey for her supper? Have we not already pledged ourselves to care for Adèle?"

"My sprite, my enchanting darling," I murmured, pulling Jane's head toward mine, and covering her in caresses she did not at first resist. "You must do as you think right, I daresay" (and thus I surrendered to my Jane almost each time there was a controversy between us). "Yet it is only right, surely, that the child should understand the other half of her inheritance," I went on, for I felt as strongly as I spoke that to deprive Adèle of her maternal family would not result in a successful ménage here at Thornfield. "Let her be educated one half the year in France," I persisted; and I felt a sense of relief that I had not had the need to mention the hallucination — as it must have been — that I had suffered when looking from the library steps out at the wicket gate.

"She came here yesterday," Jane said. "Adèle came and left a letter for us. She had intended to greet us, if briefly —" And here Jane's voice broke, and I saw she was moved. "But she could not find the courage, after being so long at school, to come and speak with us —"

"Adèle?" I said, feigning astonishment; but my dear wife, so it seemed, did not hear me. "If I could have set eyes on her once," continued Jane in a sad tone, which persuaded me further that she loved the child she once had taught, and that I would be a monster indeed to prevent her from granting a home to Adèle, "if I could have talked with *la petite*, I might have coaxed her into staying here, rather than fleeing to Paris, as she has done."

"So what can we do?" I said, secretly happy, I admit, to find the problem postponed. "If she can spend half her time in France, as I proposed, this may be a natural solution."

"Half her time in France!" cried Jane. "Do you not consider before you speak, Edward? It is how she employs the time — whether she falls into the clutches of the woman, disgraceful and decadent in every way — the woman who sent letters to you demanding money in return for not divulging details of the duel in Paris, and your present whereabouts, to the French police —"

"Jenny Colon," I said, as angry now at having to say the name of that devil's whore as Jane was at my apparent insensitivity to Adèle's situation.

"Yes, Jenny Colon," said Jane. "Do you wish little Adèle to be reared by that monster half the year?"

At this I had to fall silent. As we sat, in great animosity I must with a heavy heart report — for I foresee this type of altercation between Jane and myself, whenever the subject of Adèle Varens comes up — our mutual disagreement was tempered by the sight of John as he came down the laurel walk toward us.

"What can John want?" exclaimed my wife and I together. And we smiled at each other, at last; although, as I have to report with the deepest gloom and apprehension, the news contained in the letter the faithful John handed to me was of a nature that dwarfed all disagreements over the future of a little French girl.

"What is it, Edward?" Jane was alarmed, yet I could not confide in her. I read the brief missive twice and folded it carefully before placing it in my wallet. "Is there a reply to be sent to the authorities?" asked John. "The sergeant requests that you report to him within twenty-four hours at Whitcross."

"What is it?" Jane cried again as I informed John in a manner of great hauteur that he may instruct the sergeant to expect my attendance on him later in the day. And later, when the figure of John had disappeared at the end of the laurel walk, I rose and Jane rose with me. I was conscious, as we stood stiffly there together, that the split chestnut tree stood behind us, making a mockery of our marriage and our new-found happiness. We were no painting, of a landowner and his wife, prosperous and contented, a past and future of respect from neighbors, family, and friends written on our countenances; we were, though my darling wife did not know it yet, pariahs and outcasts forever in the country.

"It was nothing of consequence," I said to Jane as we strolled up the laurel walk to the house. "A bailiff on the outer Millcote farm who has absconded with the rents, a goodly sum."

Before Jane could comment, I went on: "I have been considering, my love, your concern for little Adèle. She has run away to Paris at a tender, even dangerous, age. I propose that I go in search of her there and return her safe and sound to Thornfield Hall."

As Jane looked up at me in gratitude and adoration, I walked on as if in a dream. I knew I could not hide the contents of the letter from the world for long.

Hideously shrunk and desiccated, dead at least five years, the body of Antoinette had been discovered in a field near Whitcross, not half a mile from here. They came to plow, and cleared a dump of turnip heads and other silage in readiness for the furrowing of the earth. They found an arm outstretched, thin and pale as a tuber grown from the rotting heap. The woman buried in Thornfield churchyard and commemorated as Bertha Mason Rochester had lost all trace of her identity when claimed from the calamity of fire and fall. This woman, though they did not know yet who she was — only that she was found on my land — was the true Bertha, my Antoinette. The locket found about her neck and enclosed in the letter showed her thus — Antoinette as she was when young, the star of the islands of flame flowers and spices, the loving, dark-eyed Antoinette of our days together, who will live forever in my heart.

★ ★ ★

And I who failed to care for the bride of my younger days — why did I not even have the courage, after the last escape of poor Antoinette from her miserable confinement, to discover if she was alive or dead? (Though as the months passed, I knew she must be dead, dead!) While I kept Grace Poole in my employ, I could believe that nothing had changed at Thornfield, and that my wife lived on the third story still; I had no heart in me to go up there and see the truth for myself. Oh, we needed the fire that would flush out the truth and leave me a widower, free to marry Jane! Yet now I shall be revealed to my sweet wife as cheat and coward, and thus complicit in the death of Antoinette.

So, Jane, what do you think of me now? You stand pale in the room where my family portraits, a roaring fire, and my faithful Pilot asleep on the hearth before it give all the semblances of a blameless, prosperous life. Yet now you know differently; I have been lying to you, so you must believe, all along. My wife, Antoinette, did not perish in the fire at Thornfield Hall. You stand before me and you tremble — you who stayed all night by the side of Bertha's brother, Richard Mason, to stanch the wounds my mad wife had administered.

But you thought then that Grace Poole was the maniac at Thornfield Hall. Do you now, as you see the truth, consider my Antoinette and myself as equally murderous, perhaps both mad, partners in a *folie à deux* of which you wish no part?

"Well, Jane," I say, as you stand twisting your hands, a habit I find hard to bear, a token of inferiority that one such as Blanche Ingram would never countenance in a member of her household. "Have you been listening to all the gossip in the servants' hall? What does Leah say of my ruthless disposal of a dead wife in a turnip field? What of old John? Is he shocked? Does he take a nip of my brandy to calm him down?"

"Not at all, sir," Jane replies, as staunch and unafraid to answer my mocking charges as she has ever been. I love her, the pang I suffer tells me that. "The servants are certain of your innocence, Edward," she continues, and always with the look of belief in her master, Edward Rochester, in her eyes for which I married her: belief in her new life as chatelaine of Thornfield Hall, whatever the disasters that may befall him; belief and trust in our happiness together, come what may.

"I thank you, Jane," I said; and it was hard to keep the emotion from my voice. "But what of the constable in the Hall who awaits my visit to Whitcross? What do you make of that?" For it did not occur to me, as I readily admit, to demand of my darling wife what she has made of the news that Antoinette had been found, cruelly interred in a shallow grave not far from the house. I knew, as I shall know to my last breath, that Jane no more considers me capable of lifting a finger against the poor wretch I was inveigled into marrying than of harming our own adored firstborn son. That those who have earned my gratitude here at the Hall should be generously remunerated for their equal belief in their master, must go without saying.

"The constable waits," Jane said in a low voice, coming up to me as if to bestow a caress — and I see, just as I am about to seize her in my arms, that she wishes not to embrace me but to speak in my ear. "He waits, Edward, but you shall take the passage from my room down into the library — and thence to the steps and the wicket gate."

As Jane whispered — and showed the extent of her trust in her husband and the father of her children, for she would lose me now, and who knows for how long? — I saw in the ormolu-framed mirror above the fireplace the door of the drawing room as it opened a crack, and John's head came around it, his eyes popping with anxiety.

"You are wanted in the Great Hall, sir," announced the good man before he left the room; and with a push in the small of the back, my wife had me by the side of the fireplace, her own slender hand pressing the panel that opens to show the narrow staircase, one of the pair built into the fabric of the house in days of conflict and civil war in the country. I tried to turn and exchange one last kiss, but this firm hand, no larger than a child's, propelled me upward, through darkness and dust. The panel swung shut behind me; and just in time, for I heard clearly, before stepping out at the head of the hidden stairs into Jane's bright, sweet room, the exchange of muffled voices, one gruff and stern and doubtless belonging to the constable at Whitcross. Jane's voice in reply — denying any knowledge of her husband's present whereabouts — spoke the last words I heard from her, for speed was now essential to me, and I took the route down the small staircase at the far end of our marital bedchamber, to the library; and thence, going fast over wet grass, to the gate where a lifetime ago (but, as I know only too well, only yesterday) I suffered the illusion that I saw Céline Varens, to be informed by Jane this morning that I had seen none other than *la petite* Adèle, grown into a young woman.

And now I go to see her again, I thought grimly. I shall be arrested, I have no doubt, for the murder of my first wife if I remain in England; while in France I am wanted for the killing in a duel of the vicomte. But I have no choice — to Paris I must go. God, and my new resolution to repair past ills, must guide me there. I reached the low gate and fumbled with a latch seldom in use, other than by myself and John when we go out on a fishing trip, the rough road that lies beside the gate leading, as it does, to a fine lake filled with roach and carp. There will be no gentle sport in coming weeks, I remind myself as I set out on this back road across my estate, a private road even the constabulary of Yorkshire would not find. I angled for other prey now; for while Jane wished me to bring back her pupil to join our circle (and hoped, surely, that the matter of the dead woman's body would be cleared up while I was fortunately absent: no awkward questions asked at the inquest, no tawdry secrets of the upper story at Thornfield Hall brought to light), I must confess that my own desire to find the daughter of Céline Varens was different. For I must discover from the child — as still I thought her to be — what she knew of the last days and death of Antoinette.

Fifteen

Adèle

The sun shines, the crowd spreads out, sprawls, enjoys itself. I walk alone, among all the people, and I feel myself at home at last. For wherever there are people, wherever a crowd gathers, as is possible only in Paris, there I may find my mother.

I think of Céline most painfully on a day such as this when the workers forget everything in the pleasure of a holiday. And while they forget, I remember: those days when Maman would take me to the fair on the banks of the Seine, and those blue twilit evenings when she would go into the hotel on the quai Voltaire and tell me to wait patiently until a handkerchief appeared at a window on the second floor, when I could go in and be with her, and not before. For Maman had business to conduct, and her red velvet purse with yellow drawstrings would be clanking with gold coins when we went back up the long boulevard to our home.

I am alone, as Nadar is too busy with his caricatures to spend time with me. "Go and inspect the booths at the parade, Adèle," he said to me — and it seemed to me, not for the first time, that this giant with red hair, if he had exhibited himself, would have made enough to keep both of us for a month. "Go and find Gérard; he has been suffering a bout of melancholy recently, it will do him good to see you." And Nadar gave me a look I am beginning to understand, now that I have arrived in the city I despaired of ever seeing again. The look shows regret at having to postpone excitement, maybe an evening on the river, a restaurant, a bottle of wine. But even Gérard, though he greets me with a sad kind of fondness, is too deep in his occult studies and his histories of the *princesse lointaine* to spare me much of his time. He gives me the look, as all Frenchmen must — but then he turns away and returns to his obsessions, just like Nadar with his cartoons and his photographs. They are not young anymore, these friends of Maman; and I hate to think she may have aged as they have done. They had time for Adèle once; they played like children, and now they send me on my own to the fair.

Twice already, I have been certain I have

seen Céline. She appears and then vanishes again, in this medley of hawkers' cries, thundering brass, and exploding rockets. I walk in the crowd, alone and possessed; and as I stare at the acrobats and the Simple Simons, their faces contorted, burned, and shriveled by wind and rain and sun, I stop to hear their witticisms and jokes, which return me to the days of my childhood, days when Maman laughed and said the comedy was as good as Molière.

Where is she now? Yesterday at midday I disembarked off the coach from Le Havre at the staging post at rue Coq-Heron and made my way across the city to Montmartre: surely Jenny Colon and the friends Maman had made in all her years in Paris would know where their *chère collègue,* the actress who could also walk the high wire and ride bareback on the circus horses, had gone in her endless search for happiness. If it occurred to me that I copied my mother, in my flight from the home I had been promised in that grim northern country where I was reared from eight years old, it did not concern me unduly. I knew that Nadar and the rest would always have a place for me, to sleep and eat and talk of the old days, which seem now so near and also far away. Are these the horse chestnut trees I walked under, with Maman and Jenny, on our way along the boulevard Saint-Germain to the stuffy flat where the old witch Cibot plied her trade? Can these pink candles, mocking my misery and loneliness, have been those that danced high in a coronet of sunbeams, above Maman's head, all those long years ago? Yet La Cibot was right, that fire loves Adèle; and as I think of her predictions, it seems that time has not moved on at all. The new distance of Nadar and Gérard will be forgotten if I go to visit old Cibot, and the truth of Maman's hiding place will be revealed. So it is, by arming myself with false hopes and promises, that I put the life that was planned for me well out of mind and — like Maman, you could say — concentrate on an impossible future.

I had known, somewhere inside myself, that the order to the nuns at Hatherleigh to release me from the seminary had come as a surprise to them. I was considered an orphan there, I must confess; only "Miss Eyre" showed interest in the progress of my studies; and the nuns wrote back to her, with reports, I have no doubt, of the continuing rebelliousness of my nature. I had convinced myself — this, too, when I was no more than the child who badgered her poor parent for a *cadeau* or a new dress whenever he appeared — that it was really Papa who wished to get in touch with me and that somebody or something — usually the nuns were to blame — stood in the way of our reunion. That the man I came increasingly to know as "Monsieur Rochester" gave less thought to the little French girl he had impulsively ordered from Paris to his battlemented house on the Yorkshire moors than to his prize dairy herd or his dog, Pilot, was a part of that grown-up truth that I, as my mother, Céline, has undoubtedly done, will spend a lifetime avoiding. How could it be that a growing woman so lovely, so clear-skinned and shapely as Adèle Varens, could be ignored, shut away in a prison such as Hatherleigh, and then left there indefinitely, forgotten? Whenever these thoughts came to me, I persuaded myself that it was Papa who wished for me at Thornfield Hall. As a father, he could not shut out his daughter from his life. Something deeper in me than anything I have confessed to before led me to believe this; and it aided me, too, in my absolute refusal of the knowledge that there was only one person in the world who would show a human heart at work, when it came to caring for the bastard of a French opera dancer.

Only Jane Eyre could have had the patience and insistence to demand my return to Thornfield Hall, these being the qualities with which she had won over the surly, arrogant man who was Monsieur Rochester when she came first to take up her post as governess. Only Jane could have transformed Papa; and it was solely to her that the lord of Thornfield and its environs would have listened, as she built up her case and pressed home her reasons for including "little Adèle" in the family.

Yet, even after the nuns had bidden me good-bye and I had traveled across the country, to alight from the coach at Millcote, I still had no idea that I would find my former governess at Thornfield. I had no evidence, it must be said in my favor, that "Miss Eyre," whose letters I was not shown — only their inquiries and comments on my scholastic progress being read out to me — was in the house of which I so often dreamed, whether as a ruin or as a home where I, a child again, would be made welcome. Jane wrote, so I thought, from her next post — indeed, I had heard Papa informing her, late on the night of the thunderstorm that split the tree by the sunken fence, that he had discovered a position for Miss Eyre in Ireland. So, ever willing to deceive myself, I saw her in my mind's eye in the green fields around Bitternutt Lodge, where Papa had sent her, exiled — as I was — for eternity.

I took the small road from Millcote, the rough stones piercing the soles of my feet through my slippers. I wished to see the Hall at its most romantic and beguiling: the wicket gate, which opened on a grassy path leading into the garden, was my chosen point of entry, and the latch worked smoothly, as I knew in my memories of it was not the case when winter gales had stiffened hinges and latch alike. I stood, my hand fumbling with the gate, and looked straight ahead, along the green path mown in long grass and wildflowers.

Papa came down the wide stone steps from the balcony beside the library door. He also looked up — as if my presence, half hidden by the low branches of the shrubs by the gate, had alerted him without volition either on his part or on mine — and he stared directly at me, as if he had seen a ghost.

I stood also quite still, and it seemed a very long time we both remained thus.

Then the French window in the library opened, and a voice cried, "Edward!" Jane Eyre stepped out. She stood a moment on the terrace, with its long balustrade overlooking the garden. But by the time she looked across at the gate in the lane, I had disappeared from sight.

Sixteen

Jenny Colon had a flat on the fourth floor in the boulevard Poissonière, a cheap district on the way to Montmartre, and it was to this temporary haven that I made my way, exhausted by the crowds, the booths in the arcades at the fair on the river's banks, where the stench of frying food overcame the delicate scents of May, and by the old men at their miserable untended stalls who sold medicines and elixirs that could bring little but nausea and fever.

I walked there, knowing I was as unwanted at Jenny's apartment — with its knickknacks from her old boudoir at rue Vaugirard, the pink pouffes and secondhand carpet, the awning I remembered sitting under on the terrace when the man they first insisted I should and then said I should not know as Papa came to visit Maman — as I had been welcome at Thornfield, thanks to the efforts made by Jane. Why, I asked myself as I climbed the stairs — these inhabited by that same Parisian smell, of dust and fried food, that I had known as a young child when visiting the children of the acrobats at the Funambules — why am I here, and why have I refused the comfort and security offered to me at Thornfield? Do I hate the poor little governess so much, who has tried from the very beginning to instill modesty, education, and decency into the *fillette* to whom Monsieur Rochester was more inclined to deny paternity than to love? Am I not mature enough now to accept the future that dear "Miss Eyre" certainly has in mind for me: as carer for her children with her husband, Monsieur Rochester, somewhere between a nursemaid and a companion; and, if I persist in my studies, eventually a governess to the daughter for whom Jane inevitably pines? Jane, as she reads the letter I left for her — it was not hard, when I arrived in Millcote, to find Leah in her milliner's shop, borrow a pen from a goggling clerk, and write a missive for the curious girl to take up to the Hall — will realize there is no way of stopping my flight to France. She will see me selecting spotted muslins for a dress, dancing at outdoor balls, and flirting with the revolutionary youths of Paris. Is this why I have come here? If only she could understand that this is not so, that already, at an age that they who knew me at

Thornfield must consider dangerous (for they heard my demands when I was small for the frivolities with which my city and my mother are forever associated), I wish only for purity and happiness. To go and seek the company of Jenny Colon, they might say, is hardly the way, then, to achieve these admirable goals. But it would have been useless, as I have known for so many years, to try to persuade Miss Eyre — or Madame Fairfax, the respectable housekeeper, or, most certainly Papa — that I come here to Paris for one last chance to find Céline. They would turn from me. The unspoken part of the arrangement, which has me contented and submissive at Thornfield as they would have had me at the wretched seminary, is the total obliteration of any trace or memory of Céline Varens. Then I may live and die in the nursery and schoolroom at Thornfield Hall, a semirelative, truly an orphan, a half ignored recipient of generosity at the hands of the master, Edward Rochester. And this, while there is still some hope of being reunited with Maman, I refuse absolutely. Even if it is now impossible for Papa to marry Céline, her daughter will be with her always, as devoted and self-sacrificing as only a fast-maturing woman such as Adèle Varens can show herself to be.

Jenny Colon stumps to the door of the flat to let me in when I make my tentative knock at the door. She does not permit me a key, and I know I must leave soon, perhaps to sleep on a pile of Turkish cushions on the floor of Nadar's studio, in my nostrils the foul stink of the fluid in which he dumps the faces of the famous; or at Gérard's, where the scuttling of his pet lobster around the floors at night will cause the hackles on my neck to rise in horror. Without a mother to turn to — without any money other than the accumulations of the frugal allowance Jane made sure was sent me from the offices of Thornfield Hall (though I did not know until the day I left the school at Hatherleigh that it was she who had made sure the money came to me, for I had no knowledge of her marriage to Papa) — without the wherewithal to survive in this cruel city, what chance have I to become other than the woman of easy virtue Monsieur Rochester foresaw? All those years ago he saved the poor child that was Adèle from the Paris gutters and had her dispatched, alone and trembling, to his castle, his home in Yorkshire. Was this in vain?

Did Adèle learn nothing of the truth of life: that those who are born with nothing will remain penniless unless they do as they are told? Maybe that is the case — the lesson is not yet understood — but even as Jenny lets me in with a grunt and settles herself back on the divan littered with copies of the *Revue des Deux Mondes* and pamphlets from the women's clubs to which she undoubtedly belongs, I swear to myself one last time that I will not give up hope, when it comes to seeking out Maman. For hints have been dropped that Céline is no longer in Italy — she has disappeared, certainly, but no one knows where.

"Maybe La Cibot has news for you." Jenny, sulky but keen to find a way of ridding herself of an unexpected guest, waggles her cheroot as she leans forward on the divan, framed in a burst of spring sunshine. I have to confess I find Jenny's own attitude to the disappearance of Céline confusing, even sad: for were not the music-hall actress Jenny Colon and the *danseuse de corde,* the high-wire dancer who wanted to become a serious actress, a tragedienne with the Comédie Française, the very closest of friends for many years? Didn't Jenny coach Céline as she poured forth her speeches from *Phèdre*? "The old witch informed me she had your cards ready for reading," Jenny goes on. "I paid her for an hour of her time a couple of weeks ago. You'll find what you're looking for with her, very likely." If Jenny didn't look me in the eye as she spoke, I no longer noticed. And that is how, without so much as a café au lait or a wave good-bye, I find myself walking through crowds — more crowds — to see the fortune-teller, the old woman who reads tarot.

Life has a way of placing both obstacles and advantages in the path of those who lose their way; maybe because the eye is sharper then and the memory more honed to long-buried events and images, the most trivial of occurrences can appear laden with significance, even with the promise of finding a new direction.

This morning in Paris when the candles on the trees began to shed their rosy petals on a crowd intent on all the pleasures of the city — a morning when I walked invisible and unanswered among the poor women with rough faces, the aristocratic women with looks of subdued anguish, and the young men in their silk cravats and gleaming waistcoats — it was clearly intended by the Fates (or, as the nuns at Hatherleigh School would have it, by our good Lord Himself) that I should not proceed immediately to the dark, stuffy rooms inhabited by La Cibot. There were other things in store for Adèle — for the child who boasts of being already a woman, but who seeks her mother and meets only the averted gaze of her friends. For it came to me that, while Nadar and Gérard and Jenny found themselves speechless when asked a simple question on the whereabouts of Céline Varens, then those who do not rely for expression on human speech may turn out to be the sole purveyors of the truth. In the case of the dogs of the boulevard Saint-Germain, the effect of their snarling, barking dance was to make me turn on my heels and walk off in the direction opposite to La Cibot's flat, to the popular revolutionary quarter of Paris, the ancient boulevard du Temple.

It hadn't been clear to me, the reason for avoiding the circus where Maman — and I, naturally, I was a child of the Funambules, petted and ignored alternately by the stars of the Arlequinade, the tumblers and clowns and bareback riders — had spent so many winters and summers all those years ago. Maman had been the most daring of the trapeze dancers; and even high up myself in the *paradis*, with the youths who were the rowdiest in Paris as they cheered and booed the exploits of the actors and dancers, silent all in their *pantomime noir*, I had to gaze higher to see Céline swinging there, a scarlet and gold comet above the crowd of spectators.

Why was it that I had come to Paris and had not called on the Funambules? Was it a dread of the mime, the crude gestures that set the cheap seats aroar? Had the love of slapstick been bred out of me by the Yorkshire seminary? It seemed unlikely: possibly I had no wish to return to scenes of my childhood, when I had so painfully just grown out of it. The kicks and assaults administered by Cassandra to the poor White Clown and the mournful expressions of Pierrot, the eternal thwarted lover, would have been, perhaps, too sharp a reminder of my own past tears and tantrums. Pierrot, in any case, would have shown me sympathy at the loss of my mother, and he would have brought another attack of self-pity to poor, lonely Adèle. The sad clown of the Funambules had always made out he nursed an unrequited passion for Maman; and he had cared for me when I was tiny, so his agonized grimaces showed, in order to gain the attentions of the beautiful Céline. The great Dubureau, already the most famous mime in Paris by the time I was sent to England, made a gesture of holding her child up to Céline every night, as she swung high in the rafters of the Funambules.

The dogs in the middle of the boulevard Saint-Germain, as they fought and leapt, took me instantly to the days in rue Vaugirard, when Jenny and Maman talked of the circus of performing dogs, Les Chiens Savants, which had preceded the new theater of the Funambules. Set between the market of Les Halles and the Faubourg Saint-Antoine, the circus contained not only dogs trained to waltz and pirouette, to jump and catch balls, and to swing on the wire in ballerina attire, but was famed for its audience, too, made up of the *canaille*, the ruffians and lowlife of Paris. Gérard would say that to use a lorgnette in their presence was to incite a riot. All this returned to me, as the crowd where I walked cheered on the rushing, swerving dogs. And when I turned and made my way to the theater where I had passed so much of my infancy and early childhood, it was the sound of the crowd, avid for the next act in the Funambules repertoire, that filled my ears and propelled me along the pavement.

"Adèle — it can't be true!" The old actor Placide was the first to see me when I pushed my way in through the doors Maman had left and returned to so often, handing her child to whichever member of the troupe happened to be standing on the step. "My God, *une belle femme!*" — and the ancient comedian chuckled up at me, for I was now taller than the character I had once revered and imitated when I was safely home, with Jenny smoking her cigar in the downstairs parlor and Monsieur Punch shouting on his perch in the ornamental cage. "For one moment — *tiens!* — I thought I was seeing not Adèle but her mother, Céline."

"Placide," I said, and as I seized him by the lapels of his ill-fitting suit, I saw him flinch and remembered that each night the character of Cassandra, played by old Placide, received a mighty cudgeling about the shoulders from Pierrot. "Where is Maman, Placide, please? This is why I've come here — to find Céline."

But Cassandra merely nodded at me. With a theatrical gesture he wiped away a tear, or a false tear (for when I was very young, the sight of weeping clowns would set me off bawling myself, and large white handkerchiefs would be produced, puddles of mock tears being mopped up, for the fun of seeing me teased and then reassured). "*Ma petite,* you must ask Duburau." The gnarled face of the simpleton Cassandra loomed into mine, so close you could see the pores thickened by years of heavy makeup. "Oh, Pierrot will be happy to see his little Adèle," Placide repeated; but now, as I saw, the shambling figure moved at surprising speed into the dark depths of the theater. "I'll tell him you're here," his voice echoed back.

I was prepared for Pierrot — my own darling Pierrot, the perpetual buffoon, unhappy lover, witless recipient of life's blows, the tender, flour-faced Pierrot — to have changed since last I saw him onstage at the Funambules, but I had not been ready for the man who stepped down from the stage in the darkened auditorium and came toward me. For a moment I held back, as the white sleeves of the famous Pierrot costume came to envelop me; then I hugged and kissed the gaunt figure as hard as I could. Pierrot did not think of me as Céline; Pierrot knew where Maman was hiding out; perhaps, a possibility I had not allowed myself to consider, Maman had in the last week or so returned to Paris, had not thought of searching for me as I did for her, and was about to perform for the great Dubureau at this evening's show. The very idea made me gasp with excitement and hope.

But Pierrot, although he offered his embraces and kisses, had none of the gaiety I remembered of the *enfariné,* the fool whose kohl-rimmed eyes looked out from a sheet-white face. Pierrot, the new Pierrot, had a grim air — and I remembered the long letter Jenny had written to me, shortly after I left Paris for Thornfield Hall. Pierrot, she said, had murdered a man — or Dubureau had; no one in this city of make-believe and cruel ribaldry could tell the difference between the actor-manager of the Funambules and the clown he played to such wide acclaim. Pierrot, in any case, had been out walking with his wife (I had trembled, as this was read out to me by the kind Madame Fairfax: had the poor wounded Pierrot, the sufferer of life's injustices, actually married Maman?), and on a summer evening, in the Paris suburb of Bagnolet, a seventeen-year-old apprentice had called out insults to him and had been struck dead by the strolling actor's cane as a punishment for his rudeness.

241

"Walking with *ta putain, ta margot,*" your whore, your slut, Jenny's letter had repeated the nature of the vile remarks; and, not understanding them, the good housekeeper had stumbled over the words as she read them out, while I shuddered at the thought that my mother, if she had indeed married poor Pierrot, had been the subject of such scurrilous attacks.

Now, seeing the man who had transformed the Funambules — and also the role of the White Clown, from a mere member of the Italian commedia dell'arte to a figure renowned throughout Europe — I saw that the murder of the young man, the subsequent trial (at which, Jenny wrote, he was declared innocent), and his own gigantic fame had in turn transformed my Pierrot into a stranger. He looked at me long and sadly as I begged him for news of Céline. His gestures, I noticed, were minimal now, and dismissive of my pleas. He knew nothing of Céline Varens: she had gone away, and that was all there was to it. Then, as if some residue of all that enormous well of sympathy shown in every lineament of the old Pierrot still lingered somewhere in this man as dedicated to silence as a Trappist monk and as conscious as a conjuror of the effect of every gesture, however minuscule, on his audience, Pierrot indicated the stage of the theater and sketched with his hands the bar of a trapeze, a horse, and a trapdoor in rapid succession. As recompense for the lack of compassion he had shown for this barely grown young woman in search of her lost mother, he offered work at the Funambules.

So it was that I entered the acting career Céline had clearly deserted, either for romantic love with her Italian musician or with the still-fervent aim of becoming a tragedienne in the manner of the great Rachel. In this theater without a license to perform speaking plays — for, as the political Nadar soon informed me, in this venue they would be considered subversive of morality and law and order — I will be a part of a spectacular show of tightrope walking, tumbling, quick change, flying traps, dancing, slapstick, and popular music — all based on the pantomime plots of the old harlequinade. I shall watch and participate in the ways ideas and feelings are shown and exchanged, when words are not permitted: and it will happen one day, I know in my heart it will, that Céline will drop by to see her old friends in the troupe and gasp with astonishment at the sight of her daughter, abandoned so many years ago, as she flies through the air on the highest trapeze.

I slept at Jenny's — she who had been desperate to see the back of me now showed a grudging respect, charging rent for a trundle bed in the corner of the boudoir and coffee and hard bread in the morning, spread with a *confiture d'abricots* with the use of a serrated knife that reminded me of the ancient cutlery at Thornfield Hall.

Apart from the occasional fleeting memory of those days, I passed dreamless nights with nothing of my strange experiences as a child in the country Jenny described as *Angleterre* with a look of profound contempt and a Gallic shrug to disturb or haunt me. The Hall, with its trees that dripped in summer and stood bare in winter, began to diminish for me, confirming the tales I had heard from my mother and her friends of the shock of a return in later life to a house that had been enormous in childhood and now appeared insignificant and small: as the days in Paris passed, Thornfield went down in my inner eye to the dimensions of a doll's house. The occupants, too, became no bigger than marionettes, dancing their way through simplified versions of their roles in that northern place: Madame Fairfax, with her snowy hair and cap, smiled and stirred the morning porridge; while Miss Eyre, who once had loomed so large in my jealous heart, was no more than a governess puppet, mouthing English verbs and going back and forth from the bookshelves in the schoolroom with atlases of the world and its oceans. In the upper regions of Thornfield, it was true, there were sudden true-to-life appearances — of Grace Poole in her high-windowed room, a mug of porter on the table between her red-mottled elbows, and of Leah as she ran endlessly up the secret stair with bed linen or ewers of hot water. But of any other occupant my unconscious mind provided no clue. The roof, clearly out of bounds, was never visited. Monsieur Rochester — to whom Jenny now did not refer: I might have gone through those years for no reason, bearing no relation to the Bluebeard I had known and feared and loved in the old days at rue Vaugirard — had apparently vanished from the home of his ancestors, along with the mad Creole wife he had brought back with him from Jamaica. Of the "friend" I had longed to make my new mother, the deluded Antoinette, there was not so much as a trace. All that would come to me — this when wide awake and practicing at the theater, often hanging upside down on the bar that was my only safeguard against a death on the circus floor — was the vivid memory of my arrival at the wicket gate by the side garden at Thornfield, where my expectations of leading a sheltered and happy life with my father had been split in two as surely as the old chestnut tree beyond the sunken fence. By the time the slight figure of Jane in her gray dress appeared on the balcony outside the library and called to Monsieur Rochester, the vision had faded into thin air — the element in which I hung suspended, before turning another somersault and gliding to the post, and then down.

I was miserable, and more homesick for my Céline than I had ever been — but I was also ecstatic in my new career, neither woman nor child as I swung and pirouetted high above the crowd. I acted five years old when, in the evening performance, I watched the specialties of the Funambules from my seat in the *paradis*: the *cascades*, which were highly complex fights with clubs and punches, a kind of ballet of insult and reprisal, ending with the famous leaping *pied au cul* — the kick up the arse — in which the tall, athletically built Pierrot excelled. Or I played for my own amusement a timid woman, a young housewife in her twenties, who gasps and stifles a sob of fear when the actors do the *sauts,* the startling and dangerous jumps up and down counterweighted trapdoors. And I'd be returned to a goggling youth again when it was time for the *trucs,* the extraordinary changes of scenery, accomplished so fast the eye refuses at first to believe them: a tall wardrobe transformed into a whale with its gaping cavern of a mouth, or Pierrot's ice cream cone, turned impossibly into a spluttering candle.

Pierrot himself, I confess, was my pride and joy. I acted any age where he would single me out for praise or admiration, whether *jeune fille en fleurs* — as he had once shown me he perceived me to be by forming a bouquet with his long, eloquent fingers, lowering his whitened nose into the blooms, and sniffing the exquisite aroma they gave off — or the infant daughter of the woman he had loved above all others, Céline Varens. I wanted to be the favorite of the great Dubureau, the silent bohemian who was king of gesture and grimace, master of the wink, the sneer, the nod, the hidden amusement, and the guffaw. I, along with the *paradis*, lived only to witness Pierrot's face.

My life was too full of the theater to pay much attention to the outside world — or even to Jenny's intense existence, concerned with politics and feminism. Coming home to the Faubourg Poisonnière and climbing the narrow, fetid-smelling stairs to the fourth floor, I'd hear the voices of her women friends, Jeanne Deroin among them, who had attempted to stand as a candidate for Parliament and had been rejected on account of her sex. Jeanne's angry tones would pierce me, tired as I was from my acrobatic stints, and I cursed the tiny flat for not affording me the space to lie down and rest in peace while George Sand was quoted, worshipped, or criticized by the women's club Jenny now organized, along with serving the radical magazine *La Revue Indépendante*. Why I didn't leave and go in search of a room where I could be alone, I couldn't tell: I knew myself to be too young still, perhaps, and the sound of Jenny's and Jeanne's thick-soled boots as they tramped along the street and up the stairs to the flat was somehow reassuring. With women like these in control, the looks, growing in number, that I received daily from men could be spat at, laughed away, or ignored. Jenny and Jeanne made a barricade against the dangers awaiting young girls in Paris.

One day it became clear that I couldn't avoid the revolution of which Nadar spoke so gravely when I went to visit him in his studio — a revolution that Jenny and Jeanne said could never take place without a transformation of attitudes toward the role of women in society. The streets were crowded; this was nothing new, to a *flâneur*, as I saw myself, one who sought out the excitement of the *grands boulevards*, the glorious thoroughfares created by Haussmann, and I kept away from the narrow alleys of old Paris. But today, as I walked in that special way, disengaged yet enchanted, a spectator rather than a buyer, I couldn't help noticing the mood of euphoria that reigned over all. Faces glowed, and people spoke of winning hard-fought rights. Light, casual dress made it difficult to tell workers from the middle class. There was a festive mood of carnival and campfires; and as I crossed the Pont d'Arcole in my wanderings, I saw columns of people with long beards and odd-looking hats marching toward me, led by a black man beating a drum. "An artist's model," said Nadar later, and he burst out laughing when I described this along with the strange spectacles of the morning: a confectioner's shop where a caricature of Louis Philippe, the king known for his umbrella and his head shaped like a pear, was depicted as a circus performer, swinging, as I did, on a high bar above a curious mob. Then there were the small groups planting a tree of liberty, with church dignitaries joining in and giving their blessing to the republic; and the dozens of deputations on their way to the Hotel de Ville, each one demanding a cure for their complaints. "The king abdicated early this morning," Nadar says as he pulls the wrinkled, frowning visages of the new politicians and their leaders from the developing fluid in the dark part of his long room. "Don't you pay any attention to the present, little Adèle?" And he looked at me tenderly, but with a sadness that makes me ashamed. How could I tell him I was bored and exasperated by the talk of Jenny and Jeanne and the shouting voice of the man who calls himself the Citizen, and whom they permitted to lie on my trundle bed all day while I am at the Funambules. "Louis Blanc is a Utopian!" "Blanqui is dangerous" "Ledru-Rollin just isn't up to the job!" — the old man's words ring in my ears long after he has been persuaded to stagger from my narrow couch and go and sit in the tiny kitchen behind Jenny's room.

"I come here to see *you*," I say quietly to Nadar; and his eyes flicker with amusement at the ease with which I slide away from the realities of history, just now in the process of being made in the streets of Paris. "You're born to be an acrobat," says Nadar, "but if you don't become part of the present, one day you'll fall off the trapeze right into it. Do you understand what I mean? What aren't you facing, Adèle? Why do you live the life of someone who no longer exists?"

I suppose I had always known this would happen one day. Now, as I go over the scene again and again in memory — the last twenty-four hours seeming like a month or a year, and sometimes much longer, when I appear to be with Nadar in his studio even before my departure for the grim, dark north of England — I see him standing as he so often does, by the sloping window in the long, raftered studio, a dripping photographic plate in his hand. He is smiling down at the emerging features of his latest sitter, but he is, I know, also looking hard at me; and I can feel my own face become a part of the artist's close scrutiny. In my half-dream, half-memory I go over to Nadar, and I look down at the plate and see myself there, the tears from my passionate grief pouring down into the bath Nadar keeps under the window so he can lie, as he tells me, and look out at the sparrows on the rooftops as he bathes. "Is it true?" I say in my memory-dream, just as I said it in real life only yesterday, the day the king left the throne of France and the republic was declared.

"Yes," Nadar says. "It is true. Your mother's friends couldn't bring themselves to tell you. Céline Varens is dead."

Of course, I imagine I'll wake up at this point. Either it's a hot day in Nadar's studio — the sun beats hard on the roof just above, and the long room bakes in summer, so the smell of the chemicals can bring on a migraine or hallucinations — or I've fallen at last from the high bar and lie unconscious on the floor of the stage of the Funambules. In neither case does anyone come to my rescue: old Placide, surely, would have rushed to see how badly I'd hurt myself; and Nadar, used to my tumbles in the old days when he looked after me for a day or more, would hardly ignore me like this. But neither the clown who plays Cassandra nor the caricaturist who now scrumples up his recent drawings of the pear-faced king as dog or leech comes to my aid.

This is how I know it really is true: it's the unbearable truth that no one can alleviate or dismiss. The death of the child's mother — I see, as I walk slowly, arms outstretched as if trying to balance, a novice on the *corde* I have trained now to obey the slightest shift in weight — I see the stern gaze of Pierrot, in his mute refusal to break the news to me. I see Jenny, absent and distant in her own state of heartbreak: for Jenny now there is no Céline, there can only be politics, revolution, change. And as I stumble into Nadar's arms I sob at last.

Nadar told me, finally, of the death of Maman. He hadn't been with her: "I heard she was ill, in Italy," he says, and averts his gaze from me, as we sit now at the long refectory table in his studio, where utopians and artists can still come and toast the future, and Céline never can be again. "I should have gone to her," Nadar says, and it is the first time I have heard in his voice remorse, he who loves the *ricanement,* the sneer at the rich and pompous, and has no space left in him for pity or compassion. "But I was so busy with all this. . . ." And he waves helplessly at the pictures of forgotten men and the caricatures of the newly famous; all, he goes on to say in a low voice, of no importance, compared to his great love and affection for Céline.

Nadar continues the story that was told him, by the Italian musician who had carried Maman away from Paris to her death. It was consumption: there hadn't been any way of stopping it, naturally. So Céline Varens, who had seemed immortal to all who knew her, like the heroines of the popular operas of the day — Marguerite in *La Dame aux Camélias* and Mimi in *La Bohème* — had succumbed to the disease that spelled ill-starred romance, and, inevitably, she had died in the arms of her lover.

When I found myself back at Jenny's flat, too numb with shock and grief to reply to Jeanne's rough greeting, it was to discover yet again that my trundle bed was occupied, this time by a youth still in uniform: red rosettes were pinned to his blue shirt, from which blood also oozed conspicuously, and his red necktie was askew, from the amateurish attempts of the women to stanch the wound. A fine belt completed the outfit, and a sword lay casually discarded in the half-collapsed tapestry armchair I recognized as having come, along with Maman's pink silk pouffe, from rue Vaugirard. "He's one of Caussidiere's men," Jeanne said, and I was also able to detect the note of admiration in the feminist socialist's voice for the working-class police force set up by the left-wing Jacobin, the new Paris chief of police. "Look, the sight of Adèle has revived him," Jenny cried. "Albert, here is our friend, *citoyenne* Adèle." So, by returning to the language of the '94 revolution, Jenny showed me she had decided on a match between the daughter of her old friend and greatest love, Céline Varens, and this son of the working classes, the people for whom, despite an obvious lack of gratitude on their part, those such as Jeanne and Jenny fought and dedicated their lives. If Adèle was to have a man, Jenny Colon indicated, then one like Albert was the perfect choice. I wondered how the two women had stumbled on this handsome and lightly wounded hero. But I was in no condition to ask politely what the origins of their discovery had been. Deep down I sensed an anxiety on Jenny's part, that my time was taken up by Dubureau, with his increasing attentions to the young trapeze artist Adèle Varens, she who draws in the crowds with her audacity on the high wire and insists the net is taken away for the final number, where she flies through the air from one swinging bar to the next.

"Albert, take some of this." Jenny smiled tenderly at the youth as she lifted a bottle of Armagnac to his lips. "You'll be fine by the evening, ready to take Adèle along after the performance, to the wedding party. Even the great Dubureau will hardly prevent you from taking an evening out on the river," Jenny went on, turning to me as if she hadn't noticed my pallor and misery — which, of course, she can hardly have missed. It's as if this wedding party — or so I now see — which Jenny and Jeanne have been talking about for days, must now preface my own union, in secular and revolutionary terms, with the young policeman, who smiles faintly up at me from my own narrow bed. We shall dance; we'll be served at the bar by the girls with puffed-up hair and blond fringes, in their striped dresses and tight bodices; we'll drink and eat until we're hardly conscious of what we're doing, or why.

"Jenny," I say, for I am determined to demand why the death of Maman has been kept so long from me, "I have come from Nadar, he has told me about Céline.

Where is she now? How could you bury her without writing to me in England? How dare you still treat me like a child?"

But my words go unheard, against a tirade of concern by Jenny for Albert's state of health and a recitation of the coming wedding-dinner menu from Jeanne — who is a *gourmande* with an appetite large enough to fuel an insurrection against the entire ruling class. "Soup, fried mackerel, beefsteak, French beans and fried potatoes, an omelette aux fines herbes, a fricandeau of veal with sorrel," Jeanne intones. "Like the dinner for our friends the honeymoon couple Louis and Marthe on the river steamer at Rouen —"

"Jeanne, we need more bandages," Jenny says. "And Albert's shirt needs laundering. He has none other to wear tonight at the ball."

"Chicken," Jeanne continues, imperturbable in her certainty that this litany of dishes will propel the trainee policeman into the arms of their *chère* Adèle. "Chicken garnished with mushrooms, obviously. A hock of pork served upon spinach, an apricot tart, three custards, an endive salad . . ."

"I'm feeling better!" young Albert delights the two women by saying. And he sits bolt upright in my bed, already with the air of a husband demanding that his dinner be brought to him.

"He's handsome, isn't he?" Jenny says as she strips the offending shirt from Albert's torso and makes for the washtub behind the screen in the corner of her room. And she winks at me as she goes, as if to insist that I plunge myself into a love affair straightaway, forgetting the fact I've just heard the terrible news about Céline.

As Jeanne brings forth another portion of the honeymoon couple's dinner, a feast she swears will be replicated tonight on the Seine in a steamer at least twice the size of the bateau hired by her friends at Rouen, I promise myself that Jenny will be forced to tell me the whole truth of the end of Céline before the evening is out.

For I need to know, did Maman say she loved Papa before she died? Did she have proof in turn, as I believe she must always have had, that Papa had loved her more than any other — that, despite his infidelities and absences, there had never been anyone in the life of Monsieur Rochester to equal Céline Varens? I need to know, and to have my instinctive knowledge of their great love for each other confirmed. Without this my life will be as meaningless as if I had never been born the daughter of either of my parents. I might as well live in obscurity, married to Albert the policeman by the dignitaries of the new republic.

And I leave for the theater, with the voices of the two women ringing in my ears as loudly as the sound I hear each day of their boots on the wooden steps leading up to the flat in the Faubourg Poissonière.

"Take care on the *corde* tonight, *mon enfant*," Jenny calls after me — and I think, sadly, that it's a little late now to show me, as she clearly tries to do, that she has understood the unhappiness I have suffered today and that she is sorry for her coldness and distance.

Jeanne's last words, as they drift down the stairs and out into the street, demonstrate the only kind of sympathy of which she is capable, that of comfort in the pleasures of the table. "A small roast leg of lamb," Jeanne sings out as I go, "with chopped onion and nutmeg sprinkled on it, coffee, two glasses of absinthe . . ."

By the time Jeanne has arrived at the cheese, the plums, the grapes, and two bottles of Burgundy and one of Chablis, I have turned the corner of the Faubourg Poissonière and set off across Paris to the Funambules.

Seventeen

They say when you drown, your life unfolds before you. Scenes that had little meaning at the time race forward to prove they are the missing parts of the puzzle you have carried within you all your life. And when your parents are gone, the puzzle looms empty and menacing: for if you are not a part of someone else's night mysteries or daydreams, you no longer have a true place in the world.

I think this was the feeling of emptiness I had when I walked down the boulevard du Temple that day. Without Céline, I was alone, no longer the *petite fille* in blue and *rose* who follows her mother in the Luxembourg Gardens; tomorrow's pantomime faithfully tracing the steps of the great actress's theater of today. Then it came to me, as consolation, that I was my mother and myself together. And by believing this, I knew at that moment, crossing the crowded street to the Funambules, hearing the roar of the *paradis* inside and imagining the jugglers and clowns as they filled in time before the curtain could rise, that I must be as Céline would have wished me to be: a tragedienne as great as Rachel, a purveyor of the deepest emotions drama and history could provide. It was my destiny to become the most acclaimed and revered actress in the land. Céline would be proud of me: from the wings, somewhere high in the sky, she would witness my growing maturity and applaud my ability to go deep into the characters I portrayed. Adèle Varens, a voice said as I climbed the steps of the theater, with its shabby pillars and the hawkers collected under the portico, each with his box of tawdry wares. Adèle Varens! People will wait in the streets to see you as you emerge exhausted and triumphant from your evening performance; Adèle Varens will become a household name!

Yet everything was as usual on the day when all had changed for me. The lion came on in his moth-eaten costume, and Dubureau handed over his bride — and the crowd catcalled and cheered as the Lovely Girl was wedded to the creature. As I stood in the crowd and observed them, I wondered what did it all mean to the child (as suddenly I saw myself, for all my pretenses to be a woman) who is about to stand shivering backstage, ready for the trapeze? Who was I now? When I began to fly, would I realize I had no identity I could call my own? Would I topple from the high wire to the ground?

And I asked myself, was flying drowning? Would all the scenes of my short, strange life come through the air and plunge me into the waves of forgetting and remembering, the deep, dark sea where I lost my mother and my father both, for he had refused to own me?

Tonight, as I watched the touching scene between Pierrot and the Lovely Girl, I felt fear for the first time at the prospect of climbing onto the bar that hangs high above the stage. As lopsided as the thin smile on Pierrot's painted face, the metal bar moves slightly in the drafts of air caused by the violent scene changes. The refusal of Pierrot's devotion by the Lovely Girl, and then the springing open and shut of the trapdoor as it swallows poor Pierrot and takes him down to hell, stirs the wire also — which is so slender only I know it is there, tormenting tonight in its demand. I walk across smiling, balancing in my little pink ballerina dress, causing shouts of "Encore!" from the crowd.

How did I ever walk over this chasm?

How can I fail to fall and break open my head?

I stand, waiting for the murmured words of support from Céline — for, since my coming to the Funambules, she has aided me in my imagination; and again and again it has been Maman, the most renowned *danseuse de corde* in the world, who has given me courage to walk without a net across a stage at least a hundred feet below. The cheers and roars from the *canaille*, who are small and far from me at the great height I walk across nightly, are as deafening as the sea.

Tonight will I dive down and down, into that thundering water?

Will I drown, in the angry jeers of a mob cheated of its glimpse of thigh and pink net ballet dress, skirt flaring as it dances across the wire?

Will Adèle die, all the sadness and happiness of her life coming to her at once in the sea of tobacco-chewing, rancid-smelling spectators at the Funambules Theater?

Where is Céline now? Knowing she is lost to me for good has robbed me of the illusion I lived with for so long — that she will come for me one day, that she will never, ever let me fall.

Trumpets blare. Pierrot, bad-tempered as a result of tripping in the understage machinery, hisses at me as I struggle to climb the pole to reach my bar. *"Vite, vite, enfant!"* and he stamps away backstage. My eyes burn, and a sudden hatred for the mime who is more famous now than the character he has created — Pierrot, Dubureau, the world hangs on the dusty tear that trickles down his cheek, the mournful arrogance with which he surveys the audience — seizes me as my legs, heavy as they have never been before, go slowly upward. Why do people say Pierrot will marry Adèle and shut her up all day in his little house at Neuilly? But then, all these past months I have smiled and preened when Placide said I was destined to be wife of the great Pierrot. Why did I do this? I hate him, I have no desire to be a prisoner of the Funambules.

But as I reach the last wavering step of the rope ladder, I understand the loss of Céline as the disappearance of the one who could, if only in my dreams, have given me the strength to run away and make a new life, without Pierrot or Jenny or all the figures from my vanished past. Now I no longer trust I can be great, without a mother to teach me the tricks and sincerity of a true actress such as Rachel. I shall never be other than what I am. And what I am is a *jeune fille sans coeur* — a girl who was born with a stone in place of her heart, a child who permitted her only friend in those friendless days at Thornfield Hall — Antoinette, the lovely, empty-eyed Creole — to fall to her death. As I will today, with no Maman to hold me firm and stop me from falling. It is God's punishment, and truly I deserve it.

The realization seizes me as I wrap my legs around the pole, striped red and white like seaside candy, a gaudy pillar of danger and impending death. I pause as the bar pulls into me. And I think, I must hang upside down like a monkey on this cruel swing, and I must fly, fly. . . .

For one second, maybe two, I pause, and the crowd, smelling my hesitation, understanding even, possibly, my new awareness of the ridiculous acts I am supposed to perform, gives a great roar of impatience. "Adèle!" They know my name by now, of course they do. *La petite princesse* of the acrobatics of the air, queen of the high fliers, a brightly dressed insect, a jeweled butterfly. As yet they are not angry with their heroine of the skies, but a few seconds more and they will be. And in their rage of frustrated hopes, Adèle will plunge to the floor of the Funambules and die.

The bar, once I'm astride, is comfortingly familiar; I could be settling, I recognize with relief, into a chair that knows my body as well as I know its strengths and weaknesses. It's nothing to somersault and drop and rise by sheer force of the arms, to the sound of applause; it's as simple today as it was yesterday. And the fear is in abeyance: I can't think further than that, but I know I have neither mother nor father while I sail, dive, and fly. I'm alone in the world and the happier for it. The trouble is yet to come — and this I know — when it is time for me to dance across the wire. So fatally, foolishly, I wait. I stay a long time on the bar — and then the shouting, insistent demands start up again. "Adèle! *La corde!* Adèle!"

And I swing back to the pole as the excitement turns to a frenzy of hysteria. Now I sense, in the crowd, their longing for my first stumble, the slip of my foot on the invisible wire that will plunge me to the stage a whole continent of terror away. The swell of sound grows and consumes me as I dock beside the red-and-white-striped pole.

It is then that I see her. I'm stepping from the bar onto the wire — which trembles at the impact of my weight as it has never done before — and I pause another fateful second, this further demonstration of my loss of nerve sending the *canaille* in the *paradis* into a cacophony of screaming. I look down — as I have been trained over many sessions not to do — and I see first, on the stage, the angry, incredulous face of Dubureau, no longer made up as Pierrot, as he stares up at me, finger wagging, his velvet jacket with its ludicrously padded shoulders heaving directly beneath me.

The sight is unbearable. I look out into the audience — another forbidden act, in the world of high-wire dancers. For everyone knows that the glimpse of a loved one — or a hated one, for that matter — can unbalance the trapeze artist. Equilibrium is easily lost: the consequences are unimaginable.

I'm on the wire, arms outstretched as if in supplication. Nobody here can think I could glide across, so violent are the twists and turns my desperate body makes, to regain its balance.

I pray for Céline to help me. But the vision of my mother does not come to me. Instead, out of the depths of my mind, there comes a picture: a dark dress, a white blouse primly tucked under it, a frank, affectionate gaze . . .

As I take sustenance from this vision of Jane, dear Jane Eyre, the governess I had considered long forgotten — and for all my denial of her, I had loved her once — I find my equilibrium returning, and, slowly at first, I make my dancing way along the wire. The crowd roars its recognition of the conquest of the force of life over death. And I smile, feeling the sweat break out along my arms and run down to my fingers as I twirl the baton I must never allow to slip away from me.

It's on my return — to the now-welcoming red and white pole and to the sound of huge applause from the spectators so far below — that I see — and, to my horror, recognize — a face in the crowd. (A real face, this: no vision from the past.)

I hesitate; my arms fly out. I almost plunge and then recover myself. I reach the pole safely and slide down. And, from the stage I run, leaping straight through the astonished crowd, and pursue what I have seen. For it is a face I know as well as my own that I saw there, a face I have no choice but to follow and find.

Part Three

Eighteen

It was growing dark by the time I had lost my quarry three times and then finally found — so I thought — the face I had glimpsed in the audience of the Funambules Theater.

First, I walked in the direction of the river. The broad back of a man in a long black overcoat, his companion a boy of about my age, had kindled the spark of recognition for which I yearned: surely, I thought as I increased my pace on the banks of the Seine, this is the answer to my long, frightening, and confusing day. This is Papa, my father come to Paris to find the child he turned away from when he married Jane. This is Monsieur Rochester — and when he sees who runs along the wide escarpment by the river, he will turn and stop, then smile down at me.

But the strange man, when at last I overtook him, bore less resemblance to the man I had come to love and hate than did the crumpled, blackened face Nadar had fished up from his tank in the old days of the wet-collodion plate. He was tall, certainly, my Monsieur Rochester, and he

271

wore a sardonic expression that had more cruelty and also less of a reflective quality than Papa's; and that he wasn't even English was soon demonstrated by his barking demand of me, in a Belgian accent, to give an account of what I desired from him, and immediately. Then, still with his young companion, he walked on.

Why I had imagined the master of Thornfield Hall with a lad of about fourteen years old, I don't know; but I was compelled, after accepting that I had blundered and followed the wrong suspect, to cast my mind back to my last moments on the high wire and to try, with all the concentration I could muster, to remember whether the dear and dreaded individual I had seen looking up at me had indeed been accompanied by a youth of my own age.

At first, the terror of the bar as it swung me high and then low across the stage of the Funambules came to me so vividly that I saw nothing but my own figure, small and determined, as it climbed from pole to strip of metal and then dropped, with a plunging movement that brought a knot to my stomach, to hang upside down over a sea of equally reversed faces.

How could I — this is how I thought on

that Paris morning as I stood gripping the stone balustrade by the Seine, hanging on in my memory as I had learned to do on the trapeze — how could I possibly recall who had been a spectator among so many today? Hadn't my grief and nervous reaction to the devastating news of Céline's death — broken by Nadar, not unkindly but with a candor that was typical of the man — unhinged me, so, my having learned of the loss of my mother, that I hallucinated my father there before me in the audience? After all, why should a man such as Monsieur Rochester, with all his estates and land, stretching far east of Millcote and west of Whitcross (and to think of those names and places filled my eyes with tears) — why should so important and preoccupied a man take the time and trouble to come to Paris to look for an orphan who had been five years incarcerated in a boarding school?

By the time I decided it was highly unlikely that Monsieur Rochester could have been in the audience at the Funambules, the Seine had lost its morning glitter and a warmth from the late spring sun had descended on the embankment and on the strolling crowds, growing in number, who had left work for a picnic or a breath of air by the river. How lucky they were, I couldn't help thinking, not to find, as I did, that they had neither mother nor father to count on — for wherever I looked, I saw contentment in the family groups walking slowly under plane trees, grandmothers and grandfathers, young parents and small children all together. How fortunate, these inhabitants of the wide boulevards and narrow, poky streets of Paris, who are not torn, as I have been, between one country and another — half of me a little *article de Paris,* a piece of frivolity and froth from this great capital, and the other a part of the dour, haunted landscape to which I was dispatched at the request of Monsieur Rochester. I belonged nowhere; and as I looked down into the gray and swirling waters of the Seine — illuminated here and there by strands of gold, as the sun dazzled through the trees — I wondered that "little Adèle," who had the courage to dance across the wire twice a day at the Funambules, now lacked the spirit to jump into the deep river.

It was the vision of the wire that in the end supplied my memory. I am walking, pert little nose upturned, as Dubureau has taught me, arms like wings that flutter at my sides, lending a false assurance of my safety. I am walking, each step a miracle of judgment and precision, in my satin ballet slippers, across the highest *corde* in Paris — and I have the audacity and folly to stare out into the faces that lie beneath and beyond my fragile form. Something — so my memory insists to me — something I don't know or understand has caused me to look out like this, gawking like a *flâneur* in the boulevard just when I should be most devoted to the accuracy of my progress on the wire.

Yet this something or someone was so powerful that a message was transmitted to me, and it was a message I desperately needed, in order not to lose my way, fall, and ruin my chances of survival.

I see in my mind's eye Papa in his seat in the middle rows of the packed theater, and I know it is no illusion. He neither smiles nor scowls: in a flash I see him in the library at Thornfield Hall, looking inward as he sits over a book or his accounts. And beside him, indubitably, is a boy. A boy who looks, I realize with a jolt of fear, like me.

Who can he be, this child who is almost a man, who smiles apprehensively up at Papa as my trembling passage across the wire begins? He is not from Papa's country

— of that I am sure. But maybe it's because he dresses in the French style, a dandy already, with waistcoat and finely cut jacket: the opposite of poor Pierrot's attempts to impress the audience with his appearance.

When the thought comes to me that the youth who seems to have taken up the affections of Monsieur Rochester may in fact be another of his children — his lost or forgotten son, abandoned as I was to a life fending for himself in the streets of Paris (and he hasn't done badly, as his costume and sophisticated manner show) — I am halfway across the *corde,* in my memory. Little wonder I had shut the idea from my mind, of Papa's real reason for coming to Paris: I would have tumbled, there and then, and broken my neck on the stage floor, if I had continued to think it one second longer. How amusing to arrive in France and take one's now-discovered son to the Funambules, to see the "little French bastard" of whom my father had spoken with such contempt to Mademoiselle Ingram! And how utterly destroying for me.

I remembered, as I held the balustrade and peered out at the river, murky now with the passing of a cloud over the sun, the effort it had taken me to expunge from my mind the possibility of the boy's birth earlier today; and how hard, too, it had been to forget my uncharitable conclusion that Monsieur Rochester, dissatisfied with the son Jane had borne him, has been happy to make contact with his French heir.

As I stood, helpless recipient of yet another dreadful possibility, a hand taps my shoulder lightly, and I wheeled around. But before I saw him, I knew the long, stained fingers to belong to my old friend Nadar; the wide-palmed hand, so patient with the plates and images it draws from the depths, in the dark-curtained area of his studio, has helped hoist me high to go piggyback down the boulevards; the cameo ring this giant's hand wears is as familiar as the face of my dear mother, Céline. "Adèle!" Nadar stoops to kiss me, and as he does so, a river steamer goes by, music blaring out across the river. The party! It occurs to me: the party Jenny and Jeanne urged me to attend, all those centuries ago, before I very nearly lost my life, stumbling and falling from the high wire. "What are you doing all alone here, *ma petite?*" Nadar demands, and I feel hot tears start up behind my eyes. I mustn't cry — so I think of

Pierrot's contrived, single tear and the laughter of the spectators at the grief of a clown defeated by his life. People love to see you cry — and so, I think as I smile back at Nadar, I simply won't! Not even, as the busy voice in my head reminds me, if I have this new possibility to consider seriously — the dreadful, life-crushing possibility that the youth with Papa had been as much a child of Céline Varens as I.

Nadar took me to the fair, as he had done over all those years when Maman was too occupied with her work onstage to come walking in the Jardin des Plantes or strolling among the peasants in from the country with their wares. He understood, without saying a word, that I needed the comfort of his presence but couldn't hear or speak, in case the sorrow flooded out and left us both unable to continue with the expedition. From time to time I tried to pass on some piece of information: that the policeman we passed with his red sash and smart uniform was one of a corps containing a young man, Albert, who waited for me on the steamer that plied its way, horns and trumpets and fiddles sounding out cheerfully; and that Nadar was missing the supper banquet of his life by preferring to take me to the fair, when he could have joined the fun. I even recited Jeanne's menu for the evening — but as I did so, my voice sank to a whisper and the real river, the river of tears I had been fighting all day, came bursting from me.

"Adèle, let's sit down and talk about all this." We were in the heart of the fair by now, and booths, filled with the brightly colored toys and curiosities of jugglers, artisans who picked a wooden puppet from the basket on the stall and brought an instant, mocking life to its jerking limbs, stood in a row like huts on a seaside pier. Some children and a lady with worn, aristocratic features stood laughing at the dancing replica of the now-deposed king, Louis-Philippe, a doll with an umbrella and a head shaped like a pear; yet Nadar, who had the kindness not to laugh, forgot his famous caricatures of the exiled monarch and hung his head in sympathy with me. "Tell me," Nadar said, "what you have not been able to speak of before, Adèle. Many times you came to the studio and waited for me to explain to you about Céline. I couldn't bring myself to tell you she was dead. But I felt, also, that a new bond had grown in you, and that you did not wish to admit it. I waited for you to come out with the truth —"

"What truth?" I cried, for Nadar now hurt me just when I least expected it. "I wanted — I want — my father —"

"No, not your father," Nadar said, and his voice was so low I could barely hear him against the shouts and hurdy-gurdy of the fair down on the banks of the Seine. "The best way is for you to tell your poor old Nadar what happened in this ogre's castle Jenny sent you to, with a strong feeling of anxiety, I have to say."

So I began, and so I told everything to Nadar, as it came to me. His eyes widened when I spoke of my discovery of Antoinette and my immediate friendship with her, and they closed in disbelief when I described the manner of death of Papa's sad wife, how I had closed the window onto the roof and left her out there. How she had desperately tried to reach the ground by way of the drainpipe down the side of the battlemented house, and how she must have fallen and died — for there was never any sign of her again, at Thornfield Hall.

"Adèle, I do not believe, even when you were eight years old, that you would do this," Nadar said, and he spoke so gravely that I realized he was earnest this time: that he did have something to tell me and that he wanted to be sure I knew the difference between truth and lies before he confided it to me. "Wasn't there anyone there, in the passage at the top of the monster's castle?" Nadar pressed me. "You know, my child, you would do better to go to La Cibot and look into her crystal ball if you want fairy stories than depend on Nadar believing your tall tales of falling mad wives and the rest."

"No, no!" I cried, stung by the assumption on Nadar's part that I lived still in the world of Sleeping Beauty, Beauty and the Beast, and the locked chamber of Bluebeard. "This was before I came back from school — before I ran away — and set fire to Thornfield Hall with my magnifying glass. The glass La Cibot herself gave me — I swear it is true! It was before the fire that *la pauvre* Antoinette fell to her death. But then everyone said she had perished in the fire. And she had not, she had not!"

Nadar burst out laughing despite himself and put out his hand to me, as he used to do when I was small and we were crossing a busy street together. "Adèle," he said softly, and as he spoke, he drew off the dark cameo ring he had worn since I knew him and touched a tiny hinge at the side, so the carnelian stone embedded in gold that lay at the top flicked back to show a portrait, equally minute, of a head engraved on ivory there. I flinched: here was Céline, as beautiful in this lifeless replica as I had known her when she was young and first flourishing in her stage career at the Funambules. Had Nadar always loved my mother? Why did he wear her ring, which never left his finger? What could it mean?

"Here," Nadar said, and with the care he lavished on the portraits of his bohemians, poets, writers, and painters of Paris, he lifted out the bas-relief of Maman, to reveal a second, even more infinitesimal picture below.

I leaned across Nadar on the dirty old bench that stood on the graveled ground of the fair, and as I did so, a barrel organ started up. The music, sad and merry at the same time, returned me to the drawing room at Thornfield Hall, where Mademoiselle Blanche had liked to play on the old pianola Papa had brought back, so the story went, from an early visit to Paris. When he was in a good mood, he'd pick me up to sit astride the brightly painted contraption and call me his "little monkey." At other times, if Blanche was selecting her tunes and smiling up at him with her velvety black eyes, he'd tell me to get out of the room as fast as my legs could carry me. Either way, the loud, indifferent music as it echoed through an empty afternoon at Thornfield Hall would bring me the acutest sense of the misery of missing Céline I thought I could ever know.

Now the pain, worse than homesickness, seized me once again. And with it came the pictures of the frightening times in Papa's house: the finding of the starving, terrified Antoinette out on the roof and the bustling figure of Madame Fairfax as she hustled me along the passage, her footsteps loud on the wooden floor after fastening the window; the dream I had had, when Jane was far from home and Papa sat disconsolate and often drunk by the fire in the library, building up the flames whatever the season; the dream of fire, caused by myself in the attic where Antoinette had for a long fifteen years been locked away; the waking to find my glass, the precious glass given me by the old witch La Cibot, missing from the box where I had stowed it. And the suspicion, from all at Thornfield Hall — housekeeper, undermaid, John and Mary — everyone except Jane. I blamed myself for the burning of Papa's house, of course I did. "Your old witch in Paris," Madame F's words would come to me when I woke, covered in sweat and shivering. "She taught you all these tricks, Miss Adèle."

As these scenes flashed through my mind, Nadar lifted up to me the picture hidden at the base of the ring. A boy and a girl were shown, painted in oils against a red velvet background. The girl, as I recognized immediately, was myself — Adèle at five years old, ringleted and pouting, the child Papa had sent for three years later, to save her from the degradation of the street. The other head was also shown in profile and was unforgettable — I, at least, had not forgotten that face, both like my own and yet nobler, with an aquiline nose and eyelashes that were long and black. I turned to Nadar; he replaced the ivory head of Céline, snapped shut the concealed locket, and slid the ring onto my finger.

"Yes," Nadar said when the loud music had died down and we could think and speak in the dusk of a fine Paris evening. "It is true, Adèle. And just as what you have told me of the pictures that came into your mind with the playing of the barrel organ have pointed the way to the truth of what happened in your English castle, so these portraits will show you who you are."

"But who am I?" I said, and as I spoke the words, I dreaded Nadar's reply. For surely — if Céline had wished me to see this ring, if she had entrusted it to Nadar with instructions I should have it after her death, then it must contain the very quality I began to see had been as concealed from me all my young life as were the tiny portraits in the cameo: namely, the truth.

"You will always be Adèle," Nadar said. "But you have a brother, who was born some hours before you, and it is he, I believe, whom you have seen today."

Nineteen

We sat silent for a long while, Nadar and I, on our bench where the cries of the old charlatan in front of his half-empty booth were broken up by the voices of skipping, chanting children and the sound of the river steamers as they came in and went out, disgorging passengers, seemed as far off as traffic from another world. The families I saw, as they passed us, unseeing and concerned only with themselves, were also distant ghosts, and those who turned their gaze, if only for a second, in our direction, appeared to expose the hidden picture of my own childhood, as just divulged by Nadar; for in each case they consisted of a mother, a father, a boy, and a girl. They had no direction, these families, save that of strolling on the banks of the Seine and showing themselves off to those less perfect than they knew themselves to be. A man and his wife, a miniature couple following in their wake, promising a future as happy and well provided for as their parents were — what else on earth could compare with this flaunted wholeness? And I, remembering myself in the days as I walked after Maman in the Luxembourg Gardens, understood at last the incompleteness we had shared; for there had been neither husband, son, nor brother in our brave procession.

Nadar showed no sign of wishing to answer the questions I had to ask. "Why did I not see my brother when I was a child? Where did he live? If Papa decided to send for me, to the dark north of England, why was the boy not included in the invitation?" Why, most mysteriously of all, did Céline not tell me of the existence of *mon semblable, mon frère,* the brother I had had to see for the first time all by myself when hanging upside down on a trapeze swing in the Funambules? Was she afraid of the consequences? And if so, why?

"You will discover when the time is right," Nadar said, and for an instant I saw the truth as Nadar fashioned it in the dark place behind the curtain in his studio, as the features of a real man or woman formed on the photographic plate. There was no room in Nadar's portraits for fantasy or speculation, he had often told me, as the lined, unblinking faces grew stronger, their identity more unmistakable as the developing fluid brought them out. Here, what you see is what they are.

Yet still I asked my questions, and the silent giant at my side shook his head at me. How did Nadar know of my "lost brother," as I saw the youth walking with Monsieur Rochester to be? Why had Céline given Nadar the ring with the locket and the cameos of her children buried deep inside? Was — was it possible even that it was Nadar who was the father of us both? That he had given his word to Céline to keep the subject to himself forever? After all, I had passed more time with the kind Nadar than I had with any other man. Was paternity the reason for the patience he had shown me over the years? And if so, why was the boy not accorded the same affection and understanding as I had been? "Adèle," Nadar spoke at last, hesitantly, as we both rose together in an unspoken decision to leave the bench, an island in the midst of the bustling world of hawkers, acrobats, and quacks selling fake medicines to the easily deceived. "The reason for my silence is . . . indelicate. I cannot speak of it to a girl, a young woman." And, as I saw, he turned away from me and bit his lip. "Go home, Adèle," he added in a low voice that was almost a whisper, as we stood together a moment outside a curtained booth where a small crowd of men had already gathered. "Go home and think no more of a past none of us can reclaim. You have the ring — I was honor bound to hand it over to you if ever we should meet again."

The fact that Nadar had not expected this to come about made my heart sink even more, and I must have looked up at him imploringly, for he went on with a brusqueness I had never heard in him: "My child, it seems to me that you are blind to the truth in this new life of yours. You spit in the face of good fortune. Go back!"

But I had heard those words, declaimed with the same urgency, many years before. Céline's voice, descending like a thunderbolt from the pink and white bedroom in . . . in the whitewashed villa by the sea, while I sat, waiting and waiting, for the time when we could all go into the sea together, Maman, Papa, and me. "Go back!" And then came the voice of the man she and Jenny said was my father — lazy, laughing, and protesting that Mademoiselle Céline Varens would last barely a month in the harsh climate of Thornfield Hall. "I'll stay here for the rest of my life if that is what it takes," came the words of the man who shared Maman's bed —

when she allowed him, that is, and Jenny was always the first to point out to me that the milord stranger had been sent packing more than once and hadn't gone into Céline's bed at all. So . . . "Where should I go back to?" I shouted like the angry child I still knew myself to be. "Where is my home?"

Nadar shook his head, and I suffered the leaden realization that I might never hear the whole story from him. "Let's go and eat at Flicoteaux, and we'll see if they have those tasty dishes you used to like," Nadar went on. "You remember how we went there. . . ." And, as if I were a new visitor to the capital of my birth, he started to describe the route to the place de la Sorbonne. "It won't take us more than twenty minutes," Nadar continued excitedly, as if the only subject of conversation between us had been routes through Paris, restaurants, and other amusements. "Come on, Adèle."

As Nadar finished talking and I stood as stubborn and mute as the eight-year-old I had now returned to being, the curtain of the booth was drawn back and a roar from the crowd rang out. More people — all these men on their own, as I was quick to see: none of the perfect families I had observed earlier, did anything but hurry past, eyes averted — pushed in among them. But Nadar frowned when he saw the spectacle that was about to begin and tugged at my arm again.

It didn't take long to understand why my old friend and protector tried to lead me away and entertain me at the students' eating house, Flicoteaux — hoping, I suppose, to distract me from the subject of family mysteries, lost brothers, absent mothers, and all the rest. In the company of young people, each looking forward to a new life, the past and its consequences would have seemed less important to me — or so poor Nadar must have hoped. Now, as I stood transfixed to the spot, I saw it was a brutal scene I was witnessing, amid the bustle of the fair. The smell of frying, which is the incense of these occasions and evokes also the domestic scent of poverty and marital desperation, grew stronger as an iron cage was revealed behind the curtain and the protagonists appeared behind the bars, to show themselves to the mob. "Very well, let me explain to you, Adèle," Nadar's voice sounded in my ears, and he spoke now with the cynicism and worldliness I had heard him use when with Gérard or

Charles, his friends the black-spirited poets who came to visit him at his studio. "That monster," Nadar continued, indicating the creature — at first it seemed hardly human — who ran into the cage, a short, stout man running behind her, "is one of those animals generally called 'my angel,' that's to say a woman. The other monster" — and I saw Nadar referred to the short, stout man who came after her — "the one screaming at the top of his voice, is a husband. He has chained up his legitimate wife as if she were a beast, and he puts her on show in the suburbs, whenever there's a fair, with the permission of the magistrates, I need hardly add.

"Pay close attention," Nadar went on, just as I shrank back from the vision I had two seconds before been so determined to stay and see. "That hairy monster has a form that possesses a faint resemblance to your own, dear Adèle. See how greedily — and perhaps she's not pretending! — she rends asunder the live rabbits and those cheeping little chickens thrown her by her keeper. And see how he beats her, this husband of hers, and snatches the prey cruelly away from her, so that the trailing entrails cling for a moment to the teeth of the ferocious beast. Such are the marital customs of those two descendants of Adam and Eve, *ma petite.* Are you certain that you wish to learn the secrets of human happiness this way?"

I turned, as sickened by this fairground display of bestiality as I had ever been by anything I'd known or half understood in my short life. I wanted only to take Nadar's arm and walk away with him to the place de la Sorbonne. I wanted the company of the laughing students; I could bear no more of the wild woman and her husband. Nadar had been right: I should have left before the dreadful cage and its occupants were shown to me.

Yet somehow I knew, as the scene on the highest floor of Thornfield unrolled before my eyes and I saw the wild, hairy creature who was in her bad times the monster who was Bertha, and not my friend Antoinette — her cruel keeper neither Papa nor Grace Poole but another, a figure so familiar I cried out, in the midst of the curious, guffawing crowd — I knew that my own curiosity had been punished by a return to the misery and solitude I had known before Nadar tapped me on the shoulder on the embankment above the Seine. For just as my horrified memory provided me with a sequence of scenes concerning the wretched first wife of Monsieur Rochester — the taunting with food among them (and later, when I was thought to have been long asleep, the cudgel blows, the whimpering, and the pleas for mercy), I saw that the hand I now sought for and grasped in the crowd was not Nadar's hand at all. A dwarf stood grinning up at me and squeezed my hand hard in return. I pulled away from him in horror and ran — but there was no sign of Nadar in all the fair, and this time I knew for certain that my obstinacy and childishness had taken my old guardian from me for good.

Now I had nowhere left to go. Jenny must be on the river with young Albert and all the others she had tried so patiently to make my friends; and I would be alone if I returned to the Faubourg Poissonière, more alone than I had ever been.

Yet a cool, quiet voice guided me as I walked, at first in any direction, and it was not my own. It told me not to panic, and even though it spoke distantly, I knew I was well advised to return to Jenny's and then to consider what I must next do. So I made my way through the boulevards to the room where a bed in the corner was — sometimes at least — home to me. But for how long I would stay there, I could not know.

★ ★ ★

Jenny was standing by the window when I arrived in the room under the sloping rafters, where today, as if in honor of the public holiday that had brought the crowds into the streets, the strong odor of frying food had accumulated and sunshine showed up the cracks in the walls, the cobwebs, and the dust. She must have been looking out for me — this I realized with a pang of guilt, an emotion I had never known in the presence of Jenny, high priestess of self-containment and doing as she pleased, regardless of the reactions of others. She had clearly sacrificed her evening of pleasure — in her case, talking with other women on the subject of freedom and revolution — on board a steamer on the river, in order to console me for the death of Céline. She had witnessed my grief and had brought her own under control. For the first time since I was a child, I felt love for the squat, aging actress as she turned from the window and came toward me: after all, she had given everything she had to Céline; and, like me, she had been abandoned for a newer, more exciting passion.

"Ah," Jenny said without any preamble, as if I had left the room only a moment before and all the confusing events of the day had not taken place. "Nadar has given you the ring, I see." And she lifted my hand and slid the signet ring from my finger. With a quick twist, she opened the locket and — as I saw in growing agitation that none of the mysteries of Céline's hidden portraits were unknown to her — she flipped up the delicate panel of gold, to reveal the tiny pictures. "And he has shown you these today?" Jenny went on in her gruff way, as if asking me if I had put powder on my hands before going to swing on the high bar of the trapeze. "You have been informed of the identity of your brother, I assume?"

"The identity?" Suddenly I was overcome by a wave of fatigue such as I had never known, even after two performances dancing across the wire at the theater. "Surely," I said, and I could hear the weakness in me as I spoke, "it is enough that I have a brother? I saw him, you know — in the audience with Papa," and some of my strength returned, at the thought that I had a true family after all, a family like those at the fair, and that my father and my brother had come to see me, dancing high above the stage.

"Yes, I followed you to the Funambules,"

Jenny said shortly, and I felt another pang, that her day plotting politics with Jeanne had been subsumed by her concern for me. "I . . . I was afraid you might fall" — and she pushed me away as I stepped closer, to give thanks for her unselfishness. "I saw them there — the milord stranger and your twin, young Lucien. But Lucien is not your father's son."

"But," I protested, "you have just said he is my twin. Lucien —" and I saw I didn't even know the name of my brother, the new member of this wonderful family Nadar and Jenny had produced for me, to make up for the loss of Céline perhaps. "Lucien," I added, and I liked the sound of the name, could imagine Maman choosing it. "Is he Lucien Varens?"

"Listen to me, child," Jenny said, and some of the anxiety and fear she must have felt for me all day was visible in her face as she came up close, the miniatures lying no bigger than jeweled insects in the palm of her hand. "Take the portrait of yourself and turn it over. Now look on the back."

It was a strange feeling, to handle the infinitesimally small portrait of the child with brown ringlets and a smiling face, who had all those long years before been "*la petite* Adèle," the loved daughter of the

297

great vaudeville actress Céline. "Now what do you see?" Jenny insisted as the picture, no more than the size of my little fingernail, showed on the back an intricate pattern inscribed in the fragile gold carapace. "Look carefully — and you will find what you want there."

At first it was impossible to make out what the swirling characters, small as they were, could signify. It was as if, I thought in my bewilderment, a child had doodled with an engraving pen on the smooth surface of the back of the portrait, in order to make an impression of a forest — or of entwining snakes — there. The letters, as I slowly saw them to be, writhed so — and were rubbed, too, with age and maybe with their frequent removal and replacement (and this, I found, I wished to believe: that Céline, for all the happiness that came to her in Italy, had not been able to bear her separation from me and so had taken my portrait constantly from the locket inside the ring) — that I could make out no more than the letter *F*, or so it seemed to be, standing tall and flanked by other shapes, all rearing and falling on either side of it.

"Yes, yes," Jenny said, and she was no longer able to suppress her impatience. "And this?" She pointed down to the minute object, and I saw at last as she did an *E,* a Greek *E* as Jane had taught me to practice writing in the schoolroom at Thornfield; then the *F,* as ornate as a peacock's feather and upright before the great *R* that followed it, turned back on itself, and swallowed the rest in the grandiosity of its flourish. *"EFR,"* Jenny spelled out for me, as if I were a small child again. "Edward Fairfax Rochester. Your Papa has given his signature of endorsement to you, Adèle. Now look at the back of Lucien's miniature. What do you see there?"

Memory is famously unreliable, and on that day, in the still-stifling heat of Jenny's room under the roof of the house in the Faubourg Poissonière, I could not have sworn that I really did remember so rapidly the coach that took us, Maman and I, to the races at Longchamps that day. I saw in my mind's eye the obsequious steward of the course and noted his haughty greeting of Céline, whom I knew at once and even at such a young age he scorned for not being a member of the aristocracy. I saw the horses lined up and heard my own screams of pleasure when the vicomte's horse romped ahead and came in as the winner.

Yes, the vicomte. Of course! I saw the coach again, on the way home, and I saw the door of the coach as it was held open by the attendant, the coat of arms resplendent in the late-afternoon sun. The vicomte's coat of arms, as gracious and arrogant as Papa's initials on the rear of my portrait, adorned that of the boy I had been told was my twin.

"Your mother was convinced," Jenny said quietly when I had gone to the window and looked out at the real world — so much simpler in its ways, as I then thought, than the tangle of the family in which I now found myself — "your mother was certain that Lucien was the child of the vicomte and you were the daughter of the Englishman who came to Paris and broke her heart, or so she would often describe him. Think back, Adèle, and you will understand why Nadar, who loved Céline too, you know, could not bring himself to tell you."

I closed my eyes, still at the low mansard window in Jenny's humble room, and I see the day at the races with the vicomte all over again, this time with the long absence of Maman and her lover, the half hour at least in which they had promised me they were finding bonbons for my delectation on the long coach ride home. I run after them, without their knowledge, and go into a covered box on the royal stand . . . and then I see them, Maman rosy-cheeked and blushing, and the vicomte with the sleek look I had come to understand in him as meaning something as good as the little sugar sweets given him by his adored Céline.

"The day they didn't take you with them to Longchamps," Jenny prompts me. "My God, Adèle, the day of the milord's terrible rage: a day you will surely never forget."

Again, though I am ashamed to admit it, it is the memory of the chocolate nuts that comes to mind: how I had wished for one and, while I was afraid of the mood the man they told me to call Papa was in, how I had had the audacity to come right up to him on the balcony of the house in rue Vaugirard and demand a bonbon from him straightaway. I hear his angry laugh as he tosses the hard almonds onto the roof of the conservatory Maman had asked him to give her, and his snort of satisfaction as the glass shatters and falls in splinters to the ground.

Then I see the coach — before Monsieur Rochester does, probably — though he must see, as I do, the expressions the vicomte and Céline wear as they disembark. Expressions that translate immediately for the milord stranger: he must know the look of satisfied desire on both their faces. But for me, I struggle to think back to the day I was permitted to join Céline and her French lover, and the picture of the box on the royal stand comes back to me, the door behind a velvet curtain, the stockings and petticoats and lace I had seen Maman donning so carefully earlier in the day, spread out over the couch at the back of the box.

Now I force myself to remember what took place at Maman's house before he threw her onto the street and wrecked the rooms as we fled weeping, to find Jenny. The vicomte was summoned to a duel — yes, that I remember very well. But Maman — how could she have let herself be seized by the Englishman and carried up to her boudoir, already half destroyed in his jealous rage? Hadn't I covered my ears, praying the ogre would not kill her as her cries echoed around a house the servants had abandoned at the first sign of coming trouble? And hadn't those cries, as I had refused to accept then, turned to moans of joy?

I remembered then how Maman had

told me with lowered eyes of the first occasion of Monsieur Rochester's seeing her with her lover — as today, they came in the coach right up to the door, thinking Céline's protector safely in Yorkshire. "Edward took the whip from the glass cabinet," Maman had said, and I remember I recoiled from her, for the first time in my life. "That was the day, *ma petite,* that you were conceived. A child of the circus, certainly."

But she hadn't told me about the other result of that first visit to Longchamps. Within the space of an afternoon, both Lucien and Adèle had been conceived. Jenny came across the room, on the unsteady boards, and stroked my cheek with her hand. "Your mother was convinced." And I hung my head, in a final acceptance of the truth. "So your brother was raised by the vicomte," Jenny went on softly, "and Monsieur Rochester took care of you. Why did you not stay there, Adèle, where you were provided for? I have not been able to understand what you are looking for, here in Paris?"

"My mother," I said, and the scalding tears came for the second time that day, to run down my dusty cheeks as Pierrot's did at the end of the evening show. "She is

303

dead, Jenny — but where is she? I need to know."

"You could have gone to see the old witch, La Cibot," Jenny replied, back to her old self, her tone tart and dismissive. "But evidently you did not."

I agreed that I hadn't thought La Cibot important — that I had left for the theater as I had no wish to be late.

"And look what you found there," said Jenny, who was laughing at last. "The witch could have warned you of things you didn't have to see while hanging upside down on the trapeze!"

"So we'll go there now," I said.

There are some faces that seem to belong so completely to the room or house they inhabit that they are barely recognizable if found elsewhere. The round table with the drooping, tasseled cloth; the lamp with the leaning shade; the curtains that would never shut out the sun even if tugged until the cheap cotton, already twenty years old, protested with an earsplitting rending sound were as much a part of La Cibot, as I remembered her, as the gray hair that was sparse on top and the bulging eyes set in a horny brow. Without mentioning the toad, the cockerel, and the crystal ball that lived under a green baize cloth on a side table also shrouded in a musty material. La Cibot, I decided as Jenny and I walked at a brisk pace into the poor district beyond Montmartre, was a fixture in my life — as well as the one responsible for handing over to me the magnifying glass with which I had conjured flames, dangerous and all-consuming, and had brought about my own banishment from Thornfield Hall. So it came as a relief to me to find that, after all the surprises of the day, there was no change in the apartment of the old witch and that she seemed to know me as well, after all these years, as she had done when Maman, Jenny, and I first visited her, in urgent need of advice on the subject of their lives — and on the future for *la petite* Adèle.

"There are deaths and near-deaths in the cards, my child," La Cibot pronounced as the tarot pack came out and the bright, terrifying images spilled out over the tasseled cloth. "*Ton père* — he is here in Paris, no?"

Jenny and I nodded together, both of us, I was aware, impatient to be told where Monsieur Rochester could be found, now that I knew myself to have been accepted by him when I was born. And Maman — I had a strange feeling La Cibot would know where she was, too, whether in Italy or here in the solemn graveyard of Père Lachaise, where Gérard had taken me once, his pet lobster tottering behind him on its string, to wander among the imposing tombstones.

"I need to know if my brother hates me," I said, and as I spoke, I felt myself blushing to the roots of my hair. For I had the right to know, surely, whether the boy with the face I saw half as my own and half as the face of the vicomte when I had known him in those far-off days in the rue Vaugirard raged in his heart against me, daughter of his father's murderer. I relived the duel as I looked into the eyes of the old witch across the table from me, and I knew she saw it also: the dawn light, the dew on the tall, stiff grass, and the two men with their seconds as they paced out the ground.

"Adèle." La Cibot reached out a hand to me, and I saw it was as brown and speckled as the toad that sat, head cocked, by a bowl of water in the darkest part of the room. "Your father did not kill his adversary. I saw it then, in the ball — the nobleman fell, and he lost consciousness, and he was taken for dead. But I saw him rise again — his eyes opened as he lay in the morgue, and he was saved." She turned to Jenny, who sat quietly on the low chair without arms, tapestry drooping from its sides and one leg missing a claw foot, so Jenny appeared to sit lopsidedly as she considered the old witch's visions. "Is the man alive, who was shot and wounded by the milord you have spoken of to me?"

"He is," Jenny assented, still in her quietest voice. "When Adèle came to Paris, I feared that her father would follow her — as indeed he has — and would find himself arrested for the murder of the vicomte."

I must have cried out then, for Jenny rose from the broken chair and went up to La Cibot, her face ablaze with triumph and joy. "You are right, Cibot! I walked right down to the rue Jacob, to the house with its long garden and the Temple de l'Amour, where my adored Céline would sit with the vicomte on a summer evening."

"Yes." I heard my own voice now, stronger that I had known it before. "And what did you see there, Jenny?"

"I looked over the wall," Jenny said, quiet as I was loud and clear. She wiped her eyes before going on. "And I saw the vicomte, and at first took him for a ghost.

For you know," she said, now addressing me with a new urgency, "once Monsieur Rochester had gone from Paris — and Céline of course had run away to the south — there was no way of discovering whether the other participant in that duel had lived or died. Only when the police came in search of your father did we assume the worst."

"The nobleman had gone to recover on his country estates," said La Cibot, and she gave a cackle of laughter. "But you, Adèle — you, too, must go home if you wish to retrieve your soul and recover your true identity. First, however, you must find and bid farewell to your mother. This is what you came here to ask me, is it not?"

"Where is she?" I said, and now for the third time that day I burst into tears and sobbed as if there would never be an end to it. "Maman is all I want, and I don't know where my home is, so how can I find her, and where should I go?"

"Wait," said La Cibot crossly as she played out the long cards on the tabletop. "It is time for you to move on — and your *pauvre mére* comes to me here to inform you that you must love a new friend now, a friend who will not take your memory of her away from you. And I am seeing now, as the cards build up their pictures of water, moon, and crossing the sea, that you will find Céline in your home here, before leaving for your home over the water."

"Home here?" I said, and I knew I sounded foolish.

"You remember where your home is, Adèle," Jenny said, and her voice was not gruff but tender. "Go there now. Go home."

I left Jenny hunched over the tarot cards with old Cibot and made my way out into the street. Dusk was falling, like the curtain at the Funambules when the clowns and jugglers, knowing that it will come down behind them, step up their acts: colored balls go higher in the air, men with red noses tumble and somersault right up to the edge of the stage, and Pierrot, walking dreamily on, receives a kick that sends him spinning into the wings.

Paris had just that air of frivolous abandon on the May evening I went in search of my father and my home. Young lovers walked with their arms about each other, under chestnut trees that snowed white blossoms on their heads. Stalls selling oysters and *oursins,* sea urchins that are balls of black prickle and succulent pink flesh, were set out on the corners of busy streets, along with flowers by the million, so the scents of roses and lilies of the valley mingled with the sharp smell of the sea. Shop windows, lit by gas from the lamps along the boulevards, promised transformation, love, and ruin with their assortment of striped silk bodices and ballooning skirts. By the river on the quai des Grands Augustins, the stalls bearing books formed an open-air library, and the cafés that spilled their chairs and tables right up to the embankment wall served wine chilled to precisely the right degree.

Everything in Paris was right that evening — except for the lost girl who walked in circles, unable to confront the past or the future, refusing to return home but wishing for nothing more in the world. For everyone out walking in the *heure bleue* that had settled over Paris, there was the knowledge of home to return to, when night finally fell. But for me, for the person known all her brief life as "little Adèle Varens," there was nowhere to go.

For it was inconceivable that the house my father had destroyed so long ago could still be there to greet and warm me as it once had done. Jealous rage had smashed first the pretty conservatory, my mother's favorite place to rest between her long, exacting roles at the theater; and had then, adding the cold calculation I had witnessed among the rich, surely sold or disposed of all the furniture and baubles once bought for her with love and joy. There could be no home for me there, whatever the witch Cibot chose to say.

Could she and Jenny be pointing me in the direction of the vicomte? Did they believe, for all the protestations made by Monsieur Rochester, and the flourishes engraved on the back of my tiny likeness, that I was truly Lucien's twin — that my sole reason for having been brought to Thornfield Hall had been an English aristocrat's whim, possibly caused by a desire to impress a grand lady such as Mademoiselle Blanche Ingram? Had all my desperate longing to be loved and properly recognized by my father been in vain?

It was terrible to think of, but I set my route from the Left Bank down the rue Jacob, and as the gloom gathered in the ancient streets of that *quartier,* I allowed my steps to slow until at last I looked over a wall, almost as tall as I, that ran around a long garden there. At the far end it was possible to see the outline of a temple; the wall was a little lower by the side of the pillared summerhouse that must have been the place of rendezvous of my adored Maman and her lover; and I stopped altogether to stare in at the curved bench that ran around the walls, and the stone table, where Maman had perhaps propped a book in order to read poems aloud, as she so loved to do.

The evening was quiet, broken only by the sound of pigeons cooing, and the peace reminded me of the countryside, when we used to go, the vicomte and Maman and I, out to the forest of Fontainebleau or Chantilly. So it made my heart leap when a figure, hardly visible in the near-darkness, rose from the bench in the farthest corner of the Temple de l'Amour and strolled, sighing, down toward the lighted windows of the house. That it was the vicomte I had no doubt: he looked older, and his right arm, in an elegant white silk sling, was held close to his body. But I knew — just as I saw the gait of his son, Lucien, in the way he walked and the line of jaw and nose as he turned to look back at the temple, as if sensing the presence of someone there, all these gestures so instantly recognizable in his son — that the vicomte bore as little relation to me as the next person walking down the street. If I am anyone, I am the daughter of Céline Varens and Edward Fairfax Rochester. This faded eighteenth-century scene — temple, old house, and all — is nothing to do with me. It is not my home.

So I go with a new purpose up to Montparnasse, the one district I have avoided in all my distraught wanderings since leaving Jenny and old Cibot. I cross the great avenue, where as a child I stood goggling at the fine ladies as they passed in their coaches. With head bent and rapid steps, like a pilgrim nearing his goal, the sacred place where offerings must be made and sins expiated, I approach the entrance to the long street that is rue Vaugirard.

And as I go up the length of pavement, as unending now as it had seemed to a five-year-old, I see our house up on the right, the high wall that protects the court-yard from prying eyes now with an even thicker growth of ivy than it had borne before but otherwise unchanged, down to the green door, slightly battered, that is set into the wall.

My heart beats fast, and with a hand that knows its way, I search for the key on the ledge, hidden from sight by the over-hanging ivy. It is there — of course it is! — and with a scraping, unwilling sound (for the key is rusty now), it turns in the lock, and the door swings open.

The courtyard makes me think at first that I have entered the wrong house after all. Instead of pot plants, the geraniums that were Jenny's proud possessions and the tall roses Maman would grow against the farther wall, there stands a tall statue in white marble, on a plinth that raises it well above human height. Clematis and honeysuckle, grown in a trellis cage around the yard, make a bower of this shrine to a goddess, and the air is heavy with their scent.

The goddess, who shines white in this last blueness of the evening, is Céline — Maman come alive and glowing — and at her feet, kneeling, head in hands, is Papa as I had known him when once we were all happy together, Papa, Maman, and I. There is no arrogance or vanity in his gaze, and he looks out at me as I enter his shrine with love and understanding. Then he rises, and comes to take me in his arms.

I cannot write here of the happiness I feel, nor of the delight the future holds for me now that we leave for England together, Papa and I.

I know only that Papa's dedication to the memory of Céline, of the house and the garden with its beautiful statue, coupled with his certain knowledge of Jane's faithful love for him, have led me at last to realize the true nature of love. Jane — the owner of the cool, quiet voice that has finally brought me here to find my past and my future — will be my companion and guide in life. That Papa loved Céline once is without doubt, and his remorse for his treatment of her will stay with him always. That I worshipped her also will remain with me to the end of my days. But, with the aid of the shy, humble girl who was in the beginning no more than governess at Thornfield Hall, we shall move forward into the next stage of our lives.

Twenty

Mrs. Fairfax

Soon all will be ready for Yorkshire's wedding of the decade, if not the century. Lilies and carnations grown in the greenhouses will be brought in, to stand in the Hall and the bridal chamber; the chapel will be adorned with red and white roses, to symbolize the two great estates at last brought together in holy matrimony. Salmon and venison are ordered, all the way from the Highlands of Scotland, while champagne and fine wines come from London.

The last weeks have been devoted to spring cleaning here at Thornfield Hall. "You must come back to us, Cousin Fairfax," said the letter from Mr. Rochester that Lord Doune handed to me on a frosty morning not so long ago (the cold there did little good to my rheumatism, and was prone to last right up to the month of May). "My wife will be happy to see you installed as housekeeper at the Hall, in the same capacity as before. Two maids, Leah and Grace Poole, are no longer with us, and you will be required to assist in engaging new staff from Sheffield or from the village of Whitcross. Please inform Mrs. Rochester of the date of your arrival: I leave for France imminently and look forward to greeting you on my return."

All the way south from the misty island of the Hebrides, I considered my plan of action on arriving at the house I had tended so long and from which I had been asked to depart in haste after the failed "wedding" of Mr. Rochester and the governess. I had been awarded a covenant, it was true: it is in my cousin Edward's nature to ensure that no relative of his shall go hungry, and I could have lived happily in retirement after leaving the service of Lord and Lady Doune. But it would have been just as much out of my own nature to refuse Mr. Rochester's kind offer of employment here at Thornfield as it would have been unlike him to allow me to live unprovided for. I accepted with alacrity and came south a month ago, to hire staff as he instructed and to clean a house left sadly in need of soap and polish, scouring rag and broom.

Mrs. Rochester met me on the front

doorstep of the Hall, just as I had come out to meet her all of seven years ago, when she had first come here to give instruction to the little French girl Mr. Rochester had placed in my care. "Welcome to Thornfield, dear Mrs. Fairfax" were the opening words of the young lady who has, since her marriage following the sad death of Mr. Rochester's first wife, become the chatelaine of this great house. "I have given you your old room and trust you will be happy to occupy it — but you will see, due to the rebuilding of the house since the fire, that a study or boudoir at the side has been enlarged and a window added, overlooking the park. We do hope the quarters will be satisfactory to you."

I curtsied by way of reply — for I admit that it was hard to express gratitude at that moment, when confronted by the reality of my poor cousin's disastrous match. This young woman — who has the air of a child still, to go by her appearance (for all that she is pregnant and not ashamed to show it), in a dress more like a girl's pinafore than the robe that would be fitting to the mistress of a noble estate — this slip of a girl then graciously wished me a very good morning and proceeded to insist on carrying my bags up two stories to my rooms.

John, the old servant who had looked after Cousin Edward at Ferndean Manor and earlier at Thornfield, refused to catch my eye when I followed her, remonstrating all the way. Miss Eyre — as we had all known her then — has brought new ways to the Hall, no doubt about it.

Today, after I have done the dining table, horribly neglected, I fear (does the new Mrs. Rochester take advantage of her husband's poor eyesight to overlook the very basics of household cleanliness?), I shall set my plan in action. After the midday meal will be a proper time to speak with my mistress — if she has her son running about the room, there is never enough attention given to important decisions. The little fellow is generally taken off fishing or walking in the afternoon, even Mrs. R, as the staff call her, being too advanced in pregnancy to keep up with a running child.

So I look once more around the red and white drawing room, gleaming now after my exertions, from mahogany side tables to gold ormolu clock on the mantelpiece, and I go to close the curtains, as I invariably do in the absence abroad of Mr. Rochester. This great receiving room, with all the treasures of his distinguished family on display, is not a suitable place for Jane

Eyre to sit in, alone. She was not born to the station required by these surroundings: she does better in the small sitting room upstairs.

There is another reason that today is the last occasion I am likely to find to speak to Madam as I must. "Oh, dear Mrs. Fairfax, I have such wonderful news," Mrs. R called to me last night as I was going up the stairs to my new boudoir. "Edward returns tomorrow, from France. Oh, cousin, he brings Adèle with him! He has found her there, as I knew he would! Shall I come in and join you a moment, while you sip your tea before going to bed?"

I do not like this type of familiarity between mistress and servant, even if I do enjoy the position of housekeeper, and my husband was a distant relative of the proprietor of Thornfield Hall. I like to keep my place, and my expression must have shown it. Besides this, as Jane must be aware, the police wait to question her husband on the true cause of the death of his first wife, Bertha, and the recent discovery of her corpse in the turnip field beyond the stables. There is little reason, as my new mistress must know, to express delight at the imminent return of Mr. Rochester to his ancestral home.

So today I tapped on the door of the modest sitting room high under the eaves of Thornfield Hall where Jane spreads her books and papers — she is forever reading and studying, though she has no reason for it, now that she is married to the wealthiest landowner for miles around (Mr. Rochester, as it saddens me to say, would be three times better off if he had done the sensible thing and married Miss Ingram, as I always prayed he would). A quiet, clear voice bade me to come in.

"Madam," I said, standing in the doorway until I was invited to sit down, as I was trained to do. "There are some matters that are left undiscussed between us. The most pressing of these is the murder of your predecessor, Mrs. Bertha Mason Rochester, by Mr. Rochester's ward, little Adèle Varens."

Jane sat staring at me, and as she failed to ask me to sit, I remained standing. "It was surely an accident, Mrs. Fairfax," the reply came at last. "If Adèle was indeed implicated, which I doubt, in the death of — of —" and she faltered again, the little impostor who has taken the Rochester name — "then the child will explain, as soon as she returns. She acted without awareness of what she did. She had no wish, in short, to do harm to — to —"

"You cannot bring yourself to say her name," I said. "But you must allow me to describe Mrs. Rochester — or Antoinette, as the French girl knew her — as she was when she first came to Thornfield. As bright as one of those moths Master Edward will say is from the West Indies when he finds it dropped from its chrysalis on the library floor, that's how she was. He loved her so passionately, you know. He swore to me, in those far-off days when we all celebrated the arrival of a bride at Thornfield, that he, Edward Rochester, would never love another as he loved his new wife. He was bewitched by her, possessed; anyone could see that."

"Why are you telling me this?" said Jane after a silence.

"Because there will be great trouble over the discovery of the body of the poor creature," I answered as clearly as I could. "Mr. Rochester, if I know him, will defend little Adèle right up to the prison door. He will sacrifice himself and make a full confession, rather than see the child punished for her crime."

Jane rose now, and I saw to my satisfaction that my description of Edward's passion for his first wife had disturbed her peace of mind at last. That is the way with the stubborn: it takes a lot to budge them from their contentment with themselves. "So you intend to speak against Adèle to the police?" she asked me.

"No, madam, I did not say that. Simply that your husband, who never loved you as he loved poor Bertha, will sacrifice himself for the French girl you insisted he bring back to you. For, after Bertha, Céline Varens was the love and light of his life. He will lose his life on the gallows" — and here Jane shuddered and clasped the child still in her womb — "when, my dear madam, you could so easily solve the problem yourself."

As I spoke, I maneuvered Mrs. Rochester over to the open window of the sitting room, only a few feet away, and placed my arm about her shoulder. "Should you not consider it, Jane?" I said. "I have your confession here, that you murdered Bertha Mason in order to free Mr. Rochester to marry you. And that, as a result of your guilt and sorrow at your wicked action, you have decided forthwith to end your life. Sign it — and you will truly free the man you love from the scaffold."

As my prisoner made no move — but, like a strangled rabbit, as I saw it, simply stared wide-eyed up at me — I decided to give a slight push to her lower body. Soon I had Miss Jane Eyre half hanging from the window. I could have let go my hold of her, there and then: she was as light as a feather, despite being with child; but for my own purposes I needed the foolish, trusting creature to sign the confession I had prepared for her before permitting her to plunge to her certain death on the cobbles of the courtyard below. It will take my dear master, as I am fully aware, a little time to recover from the violent end of the young governess he was so set on making his bride, but Edward Fairfax Rochester was born with the family's strength and determination to survive, and to increase the holdings at Thornfield whenever possible. The union with Miss Ingram has surely never been far from the master's mind, only the uncertainty as to the movements and whereabouts of the poor demented Bertha actually holding him back from making an official proposal of marriage. "You should be advised, madam," I spoke down into young Jane's face (for I do have the generosity of spirit at least to inform the self-aggrandizing little nobody of the truth of events as they took place here at Thornfield, both before and after

Miss Eyre, finding herself still to be a spinster of the parish, left the Hall, and I along with most of the other servants were sent off to find new situations). "You see, dear madam, the truth is that Bertha Mason, the first wife of your husband Mr. Rochester, did not leap from the burning battlements at the time of the great fire at Thornfield Hall. I had disposed of her in the summer when she became too much of a menace to the master's wedding plans with Miss Ingram. I shut her out on the roof, and I returned and pushed my dear mistress over the edge to her death far below — as I am shortly about to do with you, Jane. It was a matter of moments for me to run down (it was dark by then, naturally) and pull her from the bushes at the back of the Hall. She was so thin and wasted I could carry her in a sack to the field behind the hayloft, where I buried her."

"Mrs. Fairfax." Jane gasped as she struggled to regain her foothold on the floor, and I held her down firmly with a hand more accustomed to hard work, I vouchsafe, than any governess's mitt could be. "Let me go — I beg you. You forget yourself entirely."

"I shall continue," I went on, and my

tone was grim enough to silence the child-woman again — though, to do her justice, she did not shed a tear or beg for mercy as I had expected her to do. "I shall tell you all there is to know," I said, "as there is a courage in you that deserves to hear the truth, and as you are about to die. Very well: it was I who began the fire that consumed the Hall, and it was Grace Poole, not the wretched Bertha — or Antoinette, as the French girl insisted on calling her — who fell to her death from the topmost tower at Thornfield and died instantly, as you are about to do.

"For it became clear that even with Bertha disappeared — and was as time passed more and more likely never to return — Mr. Rochester still couldn't find it in him to propose to Miss Ingram. You could see why, and the scandal of his stopped marriage to you had spread through the county; and of course the first Mrs. Rochester was assumed to be living still at Thornfield Hall. I honestly don't know whether Edward thought she was still up there or not. He certainly never went up to the third story. Grace it was who gave me the idea for my plan, that dear Master Edward should be seen to be liberated at last to marry the woman of his choice. Did it never occur to you, Jane, that the majestic gait and dark tresses of Miss Blanche Ingram resembled those of Bertha — when she had been truly Antoinette, that is, on the windward island where she and her besotted bridegroom made love night and day, caring for no one and nothing but each other? Did you not see that your Mr. Rochester wanted only to repeat the ecstasies of his youth — and that you could be no more than a companion to him, a boy-girl who would fetch and carry for her master but could never satisfy him as he deserves?

"But Grace, who liked to try on poor Bertha's dresses, enjoyed her own likeness to her mistress when she put on the red dress she specially liked. (From a distance, at least; Grace was a powerfully built woman, it was for this reason that she had been taken on by the master, to restrain poor Bertha when she tried to escape.) So my plan grew, and before long I made friends with little Adèle Varens, realizing she could assist me with it. I gave her sleeping powder at night, to bring dreams she would soon be unable to distinguish from reality, and I told her, as she more and more frequently entered these states of illusion and fantasy, that her mother had written to say she would come presently, to marry Mr. Rochester and live at Thornfield Hall. Soon I had the child writing letters to herself and pretending they came from her mother, the vulgar little opera dancer Céline. She would post them in the hollow of the ash tree on the way down to the barn.

"Here it was that I underestimated the folly and greed of Grace Poole. The oaf had the notion of kidnapping Antoinette and hiding her in the barn, in the hope of blackmailing the man who has subsequently become your beloved husband. She — Grace — would keep the whereabouts, and thus the existence, of the master's wife quiet if he paid up enough for her to leave this county and go down to her sister in Devon. So I heard her, drunk as always, talking about her clever blackmail with Leah. But of course all this misfired badly. Grace, thinking she would be rich any day now, failed to keep a strict eye on the Creole — who was rescued from her imprisonment in the barn by the child Adèle. And Mr. Rochester, nervous at the uncertainty of his deranged wife's movements, did not go ahead with the designated proposal to Miss Ingram. More's the pity, I say — I would have looked after details such as the disposing of Bertha Rochester quickly enough. But luckily, all is not lost now. The Ingram-Rochester wedding will take place before the summer is out."

Jane Eyre struggled violently at my last words, and as a reminder of my superior strength and of her coming fate, I pushed her right out of the window again, her feet kicking helplessly inside the room but unable to touch the floor. "Adèle was sent away to boarding school after you and the rest of us departed Thornfield," I finished up my narrative, "so of course nobody knew that it was I who had locked Antoinette out on the roof and Adèle who thought she had been responsible for the poor woman's fall. Oh, I confess I wasn't always at my most kindhearted with the mad wife of Cousin Edward: sometimes, just for the sport of it, I'd taunt her with fresh chickens or bring the whip down on her back. But the French child Adèle, if she witnessed any of this, was too heavily doped on the potions I gave her to notice or make sense of my actions. She wept for the Creole, I know, and believed she had shut her out there to die on the roof, foolish girl.

"When the time came, and talk of the failed wedding between yourself and the master had died down, I traveled south from Doune Castle, where I was currently employed, and went to Adèle's boarding school to fetch her to Thornfield Hall. She was overjoyed, naturally, to be returning to her 'cher Papa' — but when I told her she had been disowned by Mr. Rochester and that she had nothing in the world to thank him for, she grew very quiet and sad, and it was simple, after a dose of the sleeping powder, to persuade the child that her circus wings would carry her high into the attics and that together we would experiment with the magic magnifying glass she used to boast that an old witch had given her in Paris.

"Gaining access to the upper floors was not difficult. The remaining servants thought, when they saw the old housekeeper and the child, that belongings left behind at the time of the disappointment Mr. Rochester suffered over his marriage plan with you were now to be collected. We went up unchallenged: I held the glass up to the July sun, just under the eaves where my lovely Bertha had been so long incarcerated, and the blaze was quick to start. Grace Poole, now half mad herself, lived up there like a gypsy, and old pieces of sacking, along with some of the first

Mrs. Rochester's clothes, lay scattered about and caught like tinder. When the roof of the attic started to fall in, I pushed Grace into Antoinette's red dress — horribly soiled and ripped, it hung still in the passage beyond the cell — and then I took her up onto the tower and told her to jump — 'The game's up, and the master will have you in jail, Grace,' I said, so she fell to her death, as drunk as I had ever known her, you can be sure. As for Adèle, she had run downstairs — to be caught by the flames, I hoped, for a brisk wind had got up by the west wing, and I had to reassure myself that Mr. Rochester would be out riding at this hour and not in the library, where he would suffer burns.

"As it turned out, I was mistaken there: my cousin Edward Fairfax Rochester was indeed at home — and he ran at speed up to the attic. His one idea was to rescue his first love, Antoinette. You see, Jane, she was all he cared for, in the end. And when he saw the figure standing there on the battlements, he ran to save the woman he thought was his mad wife — but it was too late. As for Adèle, as you know, she leaped to her safety — and I, too, was safe in knowing that if she told her story, no one would believe the tale of flying, the magic

331

glass, and the rest.

"Now, my dear Miss Eyre," I concluded — and as if this were all it now took to save her, I pulled a pen from the key chain about my neck and fished the sheet of paper with her "confession" from my skirts.

"All I did," I said in triumph as the wretch took the pen in her trembling fingers, as if she believed it really would save her from her fate, "all I did was attempt to ensure that the coast was clear at last for Mr. Rochester's marriage to the heiress Blanche Ingram. I had to make it all safe for the announcement of the wedding plans. But the announcement never came, and he turned to you."

"No!" came the cry from Jane as she dangled fifty feet above the driveway to Thornfield Hall. "No, I will not sign whatever you do to me. Never!"

And as my grip slackened at the sound of horses' hooves on the long drive under the trees — and as I saw a coach appear far down the road by the lodge and my captive fell back sobbing and shaking onto the floor of the room, I knew there was only one thing left to do.

The Rochester family coach had passed

by the lodge at the gateway to the estate of Thornfield Hall — and had stopped there a minute or so, for the lodgekeeper's wife to run out with tears in her eyes to greet Miss Adèle, thought lost abroad and now safely brought home — and then proceeded at a slow pace up the drive. The horses were tired from their long journey from Liverpool; the ferry bringing Mr. Rochester and his daughter from France had docked nearly two hours late, and the coachman, with the battlements and chimneys of the Hall now in sight, sat back at the reins with his eyes half closed, in anticipation of the hot grog Mary would prepare for him in the kitchen.

Adèle and her father had spoken earnestly and at length during their time together, and each now understood a new happiness, gleaned from mutual forgiveness. For Edward Rochester knew, at last, the loneliness and uncertainty suffered by the child he had summoned so imperiously to Thornfield Hall, and he had begged Adèle's forgiveness for his indifference to her in those crucial years. Adèle, in turn, was able to express her sorrow for Mr. Rochester, in his impossible marriage; had not she, too, loved the Creole and seen her become a stranger overnight? So a comfortable silence reigned in the coach, as the last familiar milestones on the road were passed.

It was Sam, the young lad who stood guard at the rear of the coach, who first saw the glow in the sky above Thornfield. He had been instructed to look right and left as they proceeded up the drive for signs of animals — in most cases, the fox — causing damage to the fencing on either side of the road. He was to report later if the rabbit trap, a rectangular hole in the road with two iron tracks placed over it for vehicles, contained an unusual number of rabbits and hedgehogs. It was unlikely, therefore, that Sam, whose eyes were trained at a low level, would note anything out of the ordinary in the sky. Only a breeze bearing grass pollen and causing him to throw back his head and sneeze led to the boy's view of the fire.

Adèle was the next to look out from the coach, and at first, believing that evening had already descended on this northern moor, and that the colors belonged to an early sunset, she let out a whoop of joy. "Look, Papa, a red sky! It will be fine tomorrow! Now, shall we go to Millcote Pond, or up on the moor to see if the plovers have nested? However busy you are,

Papa, let us go, you and me and Jane!"

Before there was time for a warning to be issued to the passengers, John the coachman had heard young Sam's cry, and the horses were whipped to a gallop. But the drive at Thornfield was over a mile long, and by the time the coach was halfway up the gradual climb and over the rabbit trap, the upper story of the Hall was well and truly alight. Now came the smell of burning and the sound of crackling flames as they consumed beams and plaster alike. The rosy glow high above turned to a deep orange and a vile smoke, choking breath and causing eyes to smart and weep, belched down toward the arriving party.

"Jane . . . Jane!" Mr. Rochester, who had seized the fresher of the two horses, galloped ahead and into the courtyard of Thornfield Hall. Adèle, leaping from the coach, ran after him. Visibility, becoming by the second less and less, vanished altogether with the first crash of falling masonry; but once the air had cleared slightly, the danger of standing directly below the blaze of the third story became more evident. For a woman could be seen there, standing by an open window, and to move or be seen, all of fifty feet below, might cause the figure to jump or to fall.

"Is it Jane?" came Mr. Rochester's anguished shout. "Jane! Do nothing until I come!"

But, as Adèle screamed in fear, the woman leaped from the window and landed amid the smoldering rubble in the courtyard of Thornfield Hall. And now, barely visible in the pall of smoke, the small, unassuming figure of Jane Eyre ran out of the house and down the steps and went straight to her. Before she could reach the body, she was caught roughly into the arms of Mr. Rochester — while Adèle, running across the courtyard, cried out in horror at the sight of the good housekeeper, Mrs. Fairfax, lying dead.

It was said later that the reason Thornfield Hall still stood after the outbreak of one of the worst cases of arson the county had ever known was Mr. Rochester's having taken care to install a steel door between the third story and the rest of the house. The fire, for all its energy and determination to consume the whole habitation, had not been able to penetrate the barrier put up by the proprietor of the Hall. Though whether, as some wags said, this door had been erected as a safeguard in the event of Mr. Rochester's second wife's going mad, it was never known.

As for Mr. Rochester and Jane, their second son was born shortly after Mr. Rochester's return from Paris. Charges against the proud father were dropped, once Adèle's testimony concerning the actions of Mrs. Fairfax and her cruelty toward Bertha Mason during her years of incarceration was heard. Jane's "confession," written in the housekeeper's hand, was produced also as evidence of Mrs. Fairfax's insane and evil intent.

So the family at Thornfield Hall lived happily ever after; and Adèle, taken for her sixteenth birthday on a trip to London by her stepmother Jane, attended a performance of *Phèdre* in the Apollo Theatre there. The tragic heroine was played by the great Rachel — and when the performance was over, Adèle was able to introduce herself backstage as the daughter of the famous *danseuse de corde*, Céline Varens. This joyous meeting was followed by an invitation on the part of Rachel for Adèle to come and train as an actress with her in Paris in a year. This Adèle's parents, after lengthy discussion, permitted, on the understanding that Adèle's other studies were completed and approved by that time.

About the Author

Emma Tennant was born in London and spent her childhood in Scotland. Her previous novels include *The Bad Sister*, *Faustine*, and *Pemberley*. She has three grown children and lives in London.

We hope you have enjoyed this Large Print book. Other Thorndike Press or Chivers Press Large Print books are available at your library or directly from the publishers.

For more information about current and upcoming titles, please call or write, without obligation, to:

Thorndike Press
295 Kennedy Memorial Drive
Waterville, ME 04901
Tel. (800) 223-1244

OR

Chivers Press Limited
Windsor Bridge Road
Bath BA2 3AX
England
Tel. (0225) 335336

All our Large Print titles are designed for easy reading, and all our books are made to last.

61	81	101	121	141	161	1
62	82	102	122	142	162	
63	83	103	12	143	163	
64						